Illustrated **Timmi TOBBSON** Adventure

LEGEND OF THE STAR RUNNER

by **J. I. WAGNER** Illustrated by **C. FROEHLICH**

Written by J. I. Wagner.

Illustrated by C. Froehlich.

Translated into English by Tracy Phua and edited by Bradley Hall.

Book design © by freshamedia GmbH based on a layout from
BookDesignTemplates.com.

Published by freshamedia books.

Printed in the United States of America.

freshamedia GmbH
Robert-Bosch-Str. 32
63303 Dreieich, Germany

www.timmitobbson.com

www.freshabooks.com

Hardcover: ISBN 978-3-96326-770-3
Paperback: ISBN 978-3-96326-777-2
E-Book: ISBN 978-3-96326-771-0

Printed in 2019.

Get the Fan-Package for FREE!

Go to TimmiTobbson.com and get the "**Easter-Egg-Companion**", "**The Lost Chapter**" as well as the "**Numbers Cheatbook**" as PDF-files to download. For free.

Groups: Get a SIGNED Book Plate!*

Should your school, book club or any other group order ten or more copies of *Legend of the Star Runner*, go ahead and tell me (write to timmi@timmitobbson.com). Let me know how many copies were ordered and I will send you just as many book plates (stickers that go inside the book) with my real (not printed) signature on them!
*Attention: The availability of book plates is limited. Please go to www.TimmiTobbson.com to see if we still have enough left.

Get in Touch:
www.TimmiTobbson.com/im-a-fan
www.facebook.com/timmitobbson

Timmi

For those who keep a twinkle in their eyes,

love in their hearts

and daydreams in their minds.

Lilli

The Chapters

Something's Odd 1

The Secret Entrance 6

The Riddle...10

The Lost Pirate...14

The Man Who Visited Twice 20

Heavily Guarded 24

The Locked Book 28

The Deep Lake 32

The House of a Hundred Rooms 38

The Treasure Hunter 42

The Theft 46

The Lost Symbol 50

The Star Runner 54

One Man Alone 60

Trapped 64

A Pirate's Realm 68

The Plan. 72

The Darkness 78

Running Out of Steam....................................... 82

Under Observation 86

The Treasure Map 90

Under Your Feet.. 94

In Disguise 98

The Key... 102

The Secret Passage 106

The Trail of the Guardian................................... 112

The Perfect Hiding Place.................................... 118

The Last Warning... 122

New Hope 126

Lotterlulu's Treasure 130

All or Nothing 134

A Summer's Day 138

Marvin

Welcome to the World of Timmi Tobbson!

This is your adventure, first and foremost. Choose wisely to survive each challenge. The magnifying glasses indicate how Timmi, Lilli and Marvin think about the difficulty of each puzzle.

Normal: Hard: Ultimate:

This is just their opinion. Maybe you will find a puzzle easy that they find hard or the other way around.

❖ ❖ ❖

You will find hints in the back of this book that can help you in solving the upcoming picture mysteries.

❖ ❖ ❖

The solution to each puzzle is revealed in the subsequent chapter.

❖ ❖ ❖

You might find the following tools helpful, though they are not required to solve the puzzles:

Magnifying glass ❖ Ruler ❖ Pen ❖ Compass/dividers (for chapter 22) ❖ Small mirror (to make reading the hints easier) ❖ Flashlight (for reading in the dark)

CHAPTER 01

Something's Odd

"QUICK, TIMMI!" LILLI'S VOICE woke me from my slumber. I squinted into the sun. She stared down at me, catching her breath. "Get up, come on!"

I scrambled to my feet and clapped the dust off my hands. "What's going on?"

"It's about a treasure," she whispered and ran off.

Puzzled, I watched her gain distance before I took up the chase. It was summer vacation. Finally. It was still early morning but you could already tell it would be a hot day. A few moments ago I had been lazily enjoying the sun. The smell of freshly cut grass hung in the air. You could hear music playing somewhere and children laughing in the distance. Now I found myself running alongside Lilli, one of my two best friends.

"Are you kidding? What treasure?" I gasped.

"Grandpa called last night and told me to be at his place at ten o'clock sharp." Lilli's eyes sparkled with excitement. "He didn't want to give away more. I told Marvin to come too. Told him to wait for us in Grandpa's garden."

❖ ❖ ❖

When we arrived, panting, Marvin was already waiting and holding Grandpa's cat in his arms. She was completely white with the exception of two orange stripes on her tail. Rushing in like that made the cat jump and she began to kick, scratch and meow, as she struggled to escape Marvin's embrace. He screamed, dropped the cat and glared at us in annoyance. He was short, chubby, loved animals and was the other of my two best friends.

Lilli ran past Marvin, paying him no mind, and rang the doorbell.

"I did that already but he isn't opening up," Marvin said.

Lilli furrowed her brow, hammered on the door and yelled, "Grandpa!" Nothing. No reaction. "He said ten sharp," she said, out of breath. "This isn't like him."

Marvin beamed at me, eyes wide. "Did you hear? It's about a treasure."

Whenever Marvin threatened to burst with anticipation, he began to bob up and down on the spot. Sometimes he was almost hopping. Like now. It looked silly but he didn't care.

"Maybe we'll have an adventure this summer," he said, bouncing and clapping his hands.

"I guess it has already started," I answered, still puffed.

Lilli gazed helplessly at the closed door. "We have to get in there. Now!" she panted. "This isn't right."

It was really strange that her grandpa wouldn't open up, but I tried to reassure her. "Maybe he just can't hear us."

"Or maybe he went to get some cake," Marvin said.

But Lilli wasn't going to calm down. Once she had set her mind to something, she wouldn't let it go. Especially if it was about something close to her heart.

"No, no, no, we need to get in there," she muttered, pressing her ear to the door, listening for sounds from the inside.

"All the windows seem to be closed," I said. "Is there another entrance?"

"No idea," Lilli answered.

"We should circle the house and have a look," I suggested.

"Well, there's definitely another way in. At least sort of," Marvin said.

I stared at him, waiting for an explanation. He smiled back at me not saying a word. We looked into each other's eyes for a couple of seconds, then he suddenly blurted out, "Uh! And I think I saw a little lizard hiding under this stone earlier." Completely puzzled, I watched him go to his knees, peeking under a stone at his feet. "Naw," he said in disappointment. "But there's some sort of worm here."

Shaking my head in disbelief, I yelled, "How do you know there's another entrance?"

 Why did Marvin think there must be another way into the house?

You can find a hint to each puzzle in the back of this book.

The Secret Entrance

IF THE CAT HAD been able to get in, maybe we could too. We strolled around the house. The grass grew knee-high and all sorts of useless stuff lay scattered around. Old barrels, a rusty wheelbarrow, a half collapsed wooden shed. But with rays of sunlight gleaming through the treetops and bees buzzing around, the garden appeared to be enchanted.

Marvin was captivated.

"Man, this grass is high! It's like a jungle. Got to be full of animals." His eyes sparkled. "Spiders, grasshoppers, caterpillars, maybe even frogs."

"There are definitely no spiders," Lilli hissed.

"Why not? I like spiders. They do no harm. They're much more afraid of you than you are of them."

"They should be," Lilli growled.

Behind the house the grass grew even higher, reaching my belly button.

"Watch your step. Don't stomp on any snails." Marvin started to tiptoe.

Somehow I felt obliged to follow his lead while Lilli shot off ahead.

"Lilli, stop kicking the grass like that," Marvin called after her.

"Just keep getting on my nerves and you'll really see me kicking," Lilli snapped. Then she stopped abruptly, turned to Marvin and added, "Kicking your butt."

Marvin decided not to respond to that and Lilli turned the corner, walking back towards the front of the house.

"Ah, a piece of wood. I'll stay on this for a while, take a break from the grass," he said, watching me with big eyes and starting to bob up and down on the wooden plank. Something he also did when feeling uncomfortable.

"Lilli is just worried. She didn't mean it," I whispered.

"Boy, you can find anything in this garden but a lawn mower," he said.

Right at that moment, Lilli returned. "Nothing on that side either."

Suddenly there was a loud crack. The board beneath Marvin's feet had given way and he plunged into a hole in the ground. Lilli and I hurried to the opening and gazed into darkness.

"Marvin! You alright?" We heard a rumbling sound but it was too dark to make anything out.

Then Marvin coughed and when he spoke his voice was croaky. "What was that? Where am I?"

We stuck our heads into the hole. Slowly our eyes adjusted to the dim light and Marvin's contours began to emerge. He lay on his back in a pile of coal.

"Congratulations. You found another way in," I said. "We're coming down."

"Wow, I bet there are mice and rats down here," Marvin cheered.

"Will you stop insulting my grandpa? He has no rats in his cellar and his garden isn't full of spiders," Lilli yelled and slid down the wall onto the pile of coal.

Marvin still lay on his back and reached up towards Lilli. "I didn't mean to insult your grandpa."

But Lilli just glared angrily down at him as she walked past.

"She gets upset really easily," Marvin concluded as I helped him up.

We went from room to room while Lilli kept yelling for her grandpa. When we came to the kitchen, Lilli stopped in her tracks. "One thing we know for sure now. Someone was still here, not so long ago."

"What? How do you know?" I asked.

 Something in the kitchen proved Lilli's observation. But what?

The Riddle

LILLI HAD SPOTTED THE fresh foam bubbles in the kitchen sink. Someone must have done the dishes not long ago.

"But if he's home, why didn't he open up? Didn't he hear us? And someone made coffee. But your grandpa only drinks tee, right?" I said.

Lilli gazed at the half full cup of coffee, then back at us. Slowly, she shook her head.

"Maybe there is someone else in here," Marvin said quietly.

The thought gave me the creeps. Suddenly we heard a loud bang, as if someone had dropped something heavy. The sound made us jump. It came from somewhere upstairs. We all looked up at the ceiling. Marvin moved a bit closer to me. Again, a loud bang.

"What's going on?" Marvin asked, inching towards me.

"Let's find out," Lilli said with determination, briskly walking towards the staircase in the corridor next to the kitchen.

"No, Lilli!" Marvin whispered urgently.

She looked over her shoulder and called us "Cowards!" as she left the room.

I fumbled nervously for my asthma puffer, pulled it from my pocket and took a deep breath. Often when I got excited, I had difficulty taking in air and had to use an inhaler.

Marvin gave me a pitying look. "Are you ok?"

"Yeah. I'm alright. Come on, let's go."

Lilli was just about to step onto the first stair leading up when I called out to her in a low voice, "Stop, wait!"

She froze.

"Don't those stairs creak? Someone might hear us."

Lilli answered my question by stomping down hard on the first stair. "Yep. Guess they creak," she said.

"Yep, they creak," Marvin confirmed.

I rolled my eyes and Lilli shot up the stairs. "Look! The ladder to the attic is down."

We followed her to the upper floor and climbed the ladder leading to the attic. We could hardly believe our eyes. Antique objects stood everywhere. Like in a museum, but much less orderly. Old statues, vases, even a knight's armor and something resembling a treasure chest. And in the middle of it all sat Lilli's grandpa, deeply immersed in a note on a little sheet of paper.

"Grandpa!" Lilli cried, running over to him.

"Oh, Lilli!" the old man yelled in surprise when Lilli jumped into his embrace, hugging him tight. "Is it already so late?"

❖ ❖ ❖

Lilli's grandpa went on to explain how the lid of the treasure chest had caused the loud banging noise. It was so heavy he had dropped it twice trying to open the chest. He had been searching for an old key he had once hidden somewhere in the attic. Unfortunately, he couldn't remember where.

"I was afraid this might happen," he explained. "I know how I forget things. So I wrote a note to my scatterbrained self, describing where I hid the key. Just to be safe, I paraphrased the hiding place with a little riddle." He looked down at the piece of paper, raising his eyebrows. "But for the life of me, I cannot figure out what this is supposed to mean."

"Let's see." Lilli took the sheet and read it out loud.

'All alone I feel so empty. Otherwise I feel so hefty.
When I feel empty, I don't move an inch.
When I feel hefty, walking's a cinch.
But when I walk, blood may spill.
Things are much better when I stand still.'

The riddle described a hiding place in the attic. What could it mean?

CHAPTER 04

The Lost Pirate

"KUNIBERT," GRANDPA SAID AS he retrieved the key, carefully wrapped up in a cloth, from inside the helmet. "That's what I call this knight's armor."

"What's the key for?" Lilli asked.

"I will let you in on its story over a cup of cocoa. Follow me."

"It's much too hot for cocoa," I whispered to Marvin.

Marvin just shrugged. "Cocoa is yummy."

❖ ❖ ❖

The cocoa wasn't just tasty, it was also ice cold. We joined Grandpa in his cozy living room as he pointed to a painting hanging on the wall.

"This is the portrait of a pirate. Not just any pirate. A legend. He went by the name of Lotterlulu."

"Lotterlulu," Marvin repeated with big, wondering eyes.

"The great Lotterlulu was active over 250 years ago. Feared everywhere. He hoarded great riches on board his equally legendary pirate ship, the Star Runner."

"Star Runner? That was the name of his ship?" I asked.

"Right, the fastest and most heavily armed ship of its time. It could arrive and disappear so quickly, it was as if it could ride the stars."

"Star Runner," Marvin said in awe.

"Eventually Lotterlulu decided to retire. That wasn't easy to accomplish, because he was hunted all across the seven seas. One night in the year 1755, he and his ship showed up here in our old town center. Back in the day, our river carried enough water to hold such a large ship."

"Here? He showed up here?" Lilli asked.

"Right here. For three days and nights the Star Runner lay anchored and nobody could be seen on board the ship. The town folk were very upset. It was no secret the government's ships had been tracking Lotterlulu for months, but they were still a few days behind. So the people blocked the river and guarded the ship day and night. But on the third night a dense fog engulfed the town.

The guards couldn't see a thing and were somehow overpowered. When the men came back to their senses, the Star Runner had disappeared." Lilli's Grandpa snapped his fingers. "Just like that."

"But the river was closed off," I said.

"That's what's so eerie. The blockade had not been breached."

"Maybe it sunk," Marvin guessed.

"The river bed was searched. It hadn't sunk."

"What then?" Lilli asked.

"There are all sorts of rumors. If you want to find out more, you need to go find the mayor's logbook from that time in the city's Academic Archives. Regrettably, only academics are allowed in - teachers, professors, students and such."

"What's written in the journal?"

"The mayor is said to have noted every occurrence in meticulous detail. If you're going to find a clue anywhere, it will be in that journal. But it's a 250-year-old book. I doubt they'll let you enter the archives, let alone allow you to take a look at it."

"What's with the key?" I wondered.

"Ah, right, the key. My grandfather handed it down to me one day. He never explained where he had gotten it from, but I vividly remember him letting me in on its secret: The key fits into the eye of Lotterlulu's treasure."

"Into the eye?" Lilli asked.

"That's weird," Marvin said.

"It is, isn't it? That's why I can remember him telling me as if it were yesterday. And he also said the treasure is supposed to lie

'high above, under a tent of stars, on the other side of a moon'.

I guess that is not to be understood literally. The Star Runner wasn't a spaceship after all. But now, my dear friends, it is time for me to pass this key on to the next generation."

Grandpa leaned over to Lilli and slowly handed her the key. It was much bigger than the palm she held up to receive it and the end was shaped like a cross.

"If someone in our family is ever going to find Lotterlulu's treasure, it is you, Lilli. Good luck."

"Thank you, Grandpa."

"It's no coincidence that I'm handing this key down to you on this very day. Until yesterday I had nearly forgotten all about it. But then someone paid me a strange visit that Friday afternoon."

"The coffee," I exclaimed, "You don't drink coffee."

"Well observed, young man. Can you also tell me who the visitor was?"

Grandpa smiled and peered at the living room table. We all followed his gaze.

After a few moments, Marvin began to bob up and down in his chair. "I can, if I get another cup of cocoa!"

 Who had visited Lilli's grandpa the day before?

The Man Who Visited Twice

THE BOOK *TREASURE HUNT* had apparently been signed yesterday. You could tell because today was Saturday and the newspaper showed today's date. That meant Lilli's grandpa had been visited by a certain Sir Thomas London. I had to admit, I was quite impressed by Marvin's powers of observation.

"This man London is a successful treasure hunter. Just last year he discovered a sunken ship and salvaged a treasure worth millions. Then he wrote a book about it and made even more money. He is staying in the Savoy, the most exquisite hotel in town. Apart from that, he seems to be a well-mannered and knowledgeable individual. Still, I couldn't give him what he asked of me."

"The key," Lilli guessed.

"No. The portrait of Lotterlulu. He doesn't know about the key. But the portrait is just as old and since I have it displayed openly, everyone knows I own it."

Lilli stood up and walked over to inspect the painting. "What's so important about the picture? Doesn't look that old at all." You could see the upper body of the pirate, dressed in black and wearing all sorts of jewelry.

"That's up to you to find out. I couldn't find anything pointing to his treasure or the location of the Star Runner. But it has to be important. London was very eager to obtain it. When I refused he started taking photos of it. Lots of them. He left then, only to return early this morning to take even more photographs."

"He visited twice? Isn't that strange?" I asked.

"Seems he missed some details yesterday. He took the photos, we drank some coffee and he left."

"This cup is half full," said Lilli.

"Right," Grandpa said thoughtfully. "He was in a hurry all of a sudden. Speaking of hurrying - you should leave now too. Let me know if you make it into the Academic Archives."

Grandpa jumped to his feet as if he had remembered something and wanted to get rid of us quickly. He herded us to the front door like a flock of chickens. Grandpa yanked it open and much to our surprise we were faced with a stubby, middle-aged man who had been just about to knock on the door. Completely taken off guard, we all froze. Since the visitor had his fist up in the air as he stared at us in amazement, I'd say he looked the most ludicrous of us all. Just as he was about to pull himself together and say hello, Grandpa slammed the door shut in his face.

"Go, go! Back into the kitchen. And close the door."

Again we were rushed away, only this time in the opposite direction. We could still hear the man knocking, right up till Lilli pushed the kitchen door shut.

"Who was that guy?" I asked.

"What's with your grandpa?" Marvin added.

Lilli pressed her ear to the door, probably hoping to pick up some of the conversation. "The door is too thick. I can't understand a word."

"We need some sort of listening device," I suggested.

"Like what?" Marvin shrugged.

"My dad once showed me. We need a big round glass. Like the ones they drink wine from."

Marvin scanned the kitchen. "Grandpa doesn't seem to be a big drinker."

"No, but I think I saw one of them earlier." I thought hard. "Where was it?"

It wouldn't work with a cup, we needed a glass. Can you see a glass?

CHAPTER 06

Heavily Guarded

WE SCRATCHED THE CANDLE wax off the wine glass and Marvin dashed over to Lilli. He laid the edge of the glass on the door and pressed his ear to the bottom of it. Lilli looked at him as if he was out of his mind. Without hesitating, she swiftly grabbed the glass out of his clutches and did as he had done. Her eyes widened in surprise.

Marvin turned towards me and shrugged. "The glass works."

"Oh no," Lilli whispered. "Come on, we have to go. Let's take off through the cellar."

"What's happening?" I asked.

"If Grandpa sees me like this, he'll know I was listening. Follow me," Lilli said with teary eyes.

Once we were out on the street, I again asked what was going on.

"Grandpa has to leave his house. He's in debt. The police are coming tomorrow with an eviction notice or whatever it's called. They'll throw him out."

"They can't do that," I protested. "Hasn't the house been in your family practically forever?"

"We have to find this treasure," Lilli said with determination. "Today!"

Marvin and I stopped in our tracks and looked at her helplessly.

"What?" Lilli gave us an irritated look. "When we find the treasure we can pay Grandpa's debt. Come on, to the Academic Archives!"

Lilli didn't leave a shadow of a doubt about what our goal for today was. We didn't dare object.

"Okay, what have we got so far?" I asked. "Lotterlulu anchored and his ship disappeared without a trace a few days later."

"Which isn't possible because the river had been barricaded," Lilli said.

"Maybe he disassembled the Star Runner, then carried the parts past the river barricade, then put them all together again and took off," Marvin said.

"Nonsense, the treasure is still in town!" Lilli said angrily.

Some time later we arrived at the city's Academic Archives. It was an old but modernized building with huge windows reaching way up to a high ceiling. The entrance hall was bathed in sunlight. As we entered, we spotted a rather old lady sitting behind a desk and guarding the door leading to the archives. A small dog sitting at her feet pulled on its leash, tugging in our direction, sniffing at the fresh air that had accompanied us in. When we approached the desk the old lady eyed us over the thick rim of her glasses. Her face became tense and stern.

"This is no place for kids. What do you want?" she said.

We were surprised by her unfriendliness. Marvin and I were too perplexed to answer, but not Lilli.

"We have to write an essay about the archives. We won't need long."

"You'll need even less time than you think, little girl, because you're going to disappear out of my sight right this instant. This is a place for academics. That's why this building is referred to as the Academic Archives. Now go away and write that in your essay."

"What?" Lilli shouted. She was furious but tried to compose herself.

The old lady hesitated for a few seconds, all the while eying Lilli. "You may stay in this entrance area where I can see you. Ten minutes. Then you leave," she finally said.

"Thank you," Lilli replied, still upset.

Marvin and I also mumbled thank you and strolled away from the desk without getting any reaction.

"What now?" Marvin asked.

"No worries. She'll leave her desk any minute now," Lilli said, peering over my shoulder towards the old lady.

"What makes you think that?" I wondered.

 Why did Lilli assume the woman would soon leave her desk?

The Locked Book

THE OLD LADY HAD just printed a note she was likely going to hang on the noticeboard behind her desk. It read that she was looking for someone to take her dog for a walk at 11 a.m. daily. The dog appeared to be anxious to get outside, as it was pulling at its leash. Lilli had put two and two together and was sure the old lady would soon leave to take her dog outside, since it was close to 11 a.m. already, as a glance at the clock hanging on the wall told us.

We didn't have to wait long. The old lady soon got up to take her dog outside. We hesitated a couple of seconds before hurrying through the door leading to the archives. The interior consisted of a single, giant, light-flooded room filled with endless rows of book cabinets stretching up high beneath a glass ceiling. We quickly and quietly tiptoed through various rows of cabinets to gain distance from the entrance door. Then we huddled together and chuckled nervously.

"What now?" I asked.

"We find the City Journal from 1755," Lilli said.

Marvin's eyes widened as he looked past Lilli. "Unbelievable," he whispered.

We turned to follow his gaze. Like all the other cabinets, the one behind Lilli was partitioned into labelled compartments. The first label that met my eye read "City Journals 1800 to 1810". Only seconds later we had found the compartment holding the years 1750 to 1760. Since the books were ancient, they were kept behind darkened glass doors protecting them from harmful daylight. Each glass door was fitted with instruments measuring temperature and humidity. Those journals were valuable and stored under optimal conditions. I tried opening the compartment, but it was as I had feared: locked.

"Crap. We need a key."

"Double crap," Lilli said, staring past me. "This can't be good."

At the far end of the aisle, the old lady's dog stood staring at us.

"It must have gotten away from her," Lilli muttered.

"If it barks, we're done for," I whispered.

Marvin got down on his knees and reached out to the dog. It immediately started trotting towards us.

"He's on our side." Marvin smiled.

After he had petted the dog for a while, we seemed to have found a new ally. Our attention then shifted towards finding the key to the compartment that held the journal. Row by row we proceeded to sneak deeper into the belly of the giant hall that was the city's Academic Archives. When we had reached its center, we spotted the key. And we spotted hundreds more. They all hung on little hooks mounted on a huge free standing disc-shaped wall. In front of said wall was a counter and between the counter and the wall stood an elderly man typing slowly on what looked to be an old-fashioned typewriter.

"Think he will give us the key?" I asked.

"He'll throw us out," Lilli replied. "We can't take any chances. We've come too far already."

"Then we'll have to get rid of him," I said, scanning the room for an idea.

"Calm the dog," Lilli told Marvin. "He'll give us away."

The dog bounced around Marvin, throwing itself on its back and jumping back up again.

"What can I do? I think it wants to play," Marvin said.

"Look," I pointed towards the bottom of the counter. A small trashcan overflowing with balls of crumpled paper sat right next to the elderly man's feet. "Let's sneak around to the back of the key-wall. I think I have an idea."

"What's the plan, Timmi?" Lilli asked.

"I'll get one of the paper balls and toss it so the dog will go after it. The old guy will see it and go get its owner."

"Flake. Let's call the dog Flake," Marvin said while Flake licked his cheeks.

"How exactly will that improve the plan?" I whispered, a little irritated.

"It won't. The plan will work. Flake will see to it."

Lilli eyed the key guard with suspicion. "I'm not sure he'll actually see the paper ball. Or the dog for that matter."

"Why not? What is it?" I asked.

Why was Lilli sure the key guard wouldn't see Flake?

The Deep Lake

"JUST BECAUSE THE MAN is blind?" Marvin wasn't convinced. "Blind people often have a superior sense of hearing. Okay, he won't see Flake, but he'll hear him."

Lilli and I exchanged doubtful looks.

"Believe me. It will work," Marvin whispered, getting somewhat excited. "Blind people can hear almost anything. Just the other day I saw a movie about a blind samurai. He split apples in mid-air with his sword!"

"Okay, okay," I interrupted Marvin to keep him from rambling on, especially since his whispering had gotten progressively louder.

❖ ❖ ❖

A short while later I nervously tossed a small ball of crumpled paper in front of the desk. Flake darted for the ball and caught up with it quickly, but couldn't find any grip on the slippery floor and so he went skidding way past the ball, finally crashing into the bottom of the cabinet opposite the desk.

"Jesus!" The key guard shouted in surprise. "I told her not to bring that dog."

Flake quickly scrambled back up and sprinted towards the paper ball. This time the dog managed to grab it and looked quite proud of himself as he continued to slide over the smooth floor, slowly turning on his own axis and ultimately crashing into the bottom of the blind man's desk. After Flake had gotten back on his feet, he slowly trotted towards us, seemingly having learned from his high speed accidents.

"Oh no," I whispered.

"He'll lead the man right to us!" Marvin muttered, his eyes widening.

"Let's go, let's go," Lilli urged us in a low voice.

"No, he'll follow us," I said. "I'll just toss the ball back."

I reached out to the dog who was approaching with the ball in his jaws. "I'll just toss it back."

Inches before the dog had reached my hand, a big palm appeared out of nowhere, fishing Flake right up off the ground. We all froze, not even daring to breathe. The blind key guard stood right in front of us holding Flake in his arms. He had lowered his dark glasses and strikingly white eyes stared at us. Frightened, we gaped right back at him. He frowned and seemed to sniff a bit. A small eternity passed before he finally grunted, slid his glasses back up and turned on the spot to take off in a rush, most likely returning Flake to his owner. We all breathed a sigh of relief.

"That...," Marvin gasped.

"...was close," I finished his sentence and took a puff from my asthma inhaler.

"Come on," Lilli demanded, already impatient again, and tip-toed back to the compartment.

❖ ❖ ❖

A few moments later we held the treasured book in our hands. Carefully we flipped through its pages, which had become brittle and yellowed through the centuries. The writing was difficult to read but we were looking for an especially peculiar word: Lotterlulu.

And there it was!

The first entry we found mentioning the pirate was dated the 10th of July 1755. We couldn't really decipher much, but found a small piece of paper stuck between the book's pages. It was a map of the city. You could clearly tell that by the course of the river and we could even recognize several distinct streets. At the upper end of the map lay the big lake.

"Look!" Lilli pointed at the lake and followed a broad line with her finger which met the river flowing in the south. "It's a canal leading from the lake to the river."

"Yeah, the lake isn't natural. They dug a hole and filled it with water from the river," I said.

"That's why they hold the lake foundation ceremony every year," said Marvin.

"Look, the X. The book says it marks the place where the Star Runner lay at anchor. You think they sailed through the canal to the lake?" Lilli asked.

"And then he just sank the ship there," Marvin said excitedly. "The water is deep. I bet that's where the treasure is. Nobody thought to search the lake!"

"You might be right. Nobody imagined he could simply sail to the lake right through the city," I said.

"Hmm, I don't know," Lilli mumbled reading the book. "I think it says something here."

We inched closer to her, trying to read it ourselves.

"The men guarding the ship were overpowered. When they came back to their senses, each guard mounted a horse and galloped along one of the three roads that led alongside the canal or crossed it at some point."

"They searched the canal from the roads and bridges. Maybe they even got to the lake."

"Do some of the roads even lead up to the lake? Most seem to have dead ends," I said.

"Hmm, let's see," Lilli mumbled, eying the map. "These little shapes are probably houses. The book says the guards were ordered to stick to the roads so they probably didn't take shortcuts through the gaps between these buildings. The letters A, B and

C mark the starting points of the guards and these arrows show which roads they followed. And I think I know which route leads to the lake."

 Which guard might have ridden all the way to the lake in his search for the Star Runner?

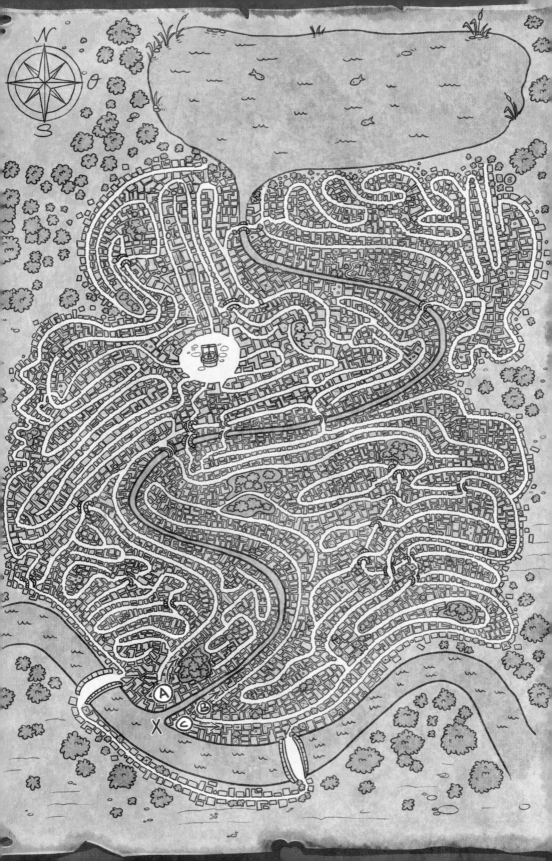

The House of a Hundred Rooms

"SO ROUTE B RUNS all the way to the lake. But the guards would have taken forever to get there and the ship could already have been sunk by then," Lilli said.

Marvin was all excited. "The lake, it's the lake!"

"But it's deep. We won't manage without help," I said.

Lilli gave me a questioning look. "Who do you think is going to help us? The fire brigade?"

I looked up. "Well, the treasure hunter," I suggested. "What was his name again? London. And your grandpa said something about the hotel he's staying at, didn't he?"

Lilli didn't need to think long. "The Savoy."

Marvin jumped up. "To the Savoy!"

"And how do we get out of here?" I whispered.

The old lady guarding the entry to the Archive sat engrossed in her papers behind her table in the lobby. She noticed us out of the corner of her eye and her face went red with rage. Before she could say anything, Lilli tossed the key to the book compartment on her desk. With a voice sweet as an angel, she said softly, "Don't worry. We won't tell anyone you were so kind as to let us in." Lilli gave her another quick smile, rocked up onto her tiptoes and down again, turned briskly and left. Marvin and I followed

Lilli, of course not without waving goodbye to Flake. The old lady looked like her head would explode any minute.

The Savoy was situated in a grand, old building. Outside, in front of the red-carpeted steps, stood a bellhop. Red flags with the hotel's logo hung on the façade.

"Let's just go in," I suggested, and we darted past the bellhop, up the stairs. But the stupid door wouldn't open. A revolving door. The bellhop turned and came towards us.

"Great, now we're done for. There must be a button here or something. Why won't it move?" Lilli said.

In no time, the bellhop was standing behind us. "Sirs, madam." Was he talking to us? "Can I help you?" It was not a question though. He held a card up to a little sensor and the revolving door began to move.

Lilli gave him an anxious look. "Thank you."

We jostled our way in as fast as we could, before he could start asking questions. Safely inside, we felt the bellhop's gaze on our backs through the glass door.

I'd never seen anything as luxurious as this enormous room. To our left was a long counter with a lady standing behind it who wore the same hotel uniform as the bellhop. A sign informed us that this was the *Reception.* Behind the counter you could see a wall full of little, numbered pigeonholes. Some of them contained letters. It was the mail for the rooms. Straight ahead you saw golden elevators and a large piano bar. The right side of the room was equipped with all sorts of seating and a souvenir shop. All over the place were guests in chic clothing.

"If we find the treasure, I want to spend the night here sometime," whispered Marvin, his jaw dropping.

"Don't be silly, what do you want in a place like this?" Lilli sounded irritated. But you could see the wonder in her eyes too.

"At least we could sit at the bar and eat some chips, right Timmi?"

"Sure, Marvin. It's a deal."

Lilli's gaze broke away from all the lavish, sparkling surfaces. "We have to ask which room the treasure hunter is in," she said, straightened herself up and pranced over to the reception.

She soon came back. "They won't tell me which room he's in. The woman said I should fill out this green entry form – they're having a sweepstake for fans. Then I might win a ticket to a private book reading next week." Lilli rolled her eyes.

"But next week's too late," I said.

"No worries," Lilli said in a stage whisper. "I am pretty sure I already know which room Sir London is staying in."

 Which room must Sir London have been in?

CHAPTER 10

The Treasure Hunter

THERE WAS ONLY ONE pigeonhole overflowing with green forms: number 307. Sir London must have been planning to draw the winner of his private reading himself. The metal detector to the left of the reception also seemed to be meant for that room. Although you couldn't actually see the first digit on the label, this seemed like a reasonable assumption.

A short while later we knocked on the door numbered 307. "Just a moment, please," we heard a voice from within. "Just a moment, I'm not as fast as I used to be."

When the door opened, an old man with a walking stick wearing old-fashioned clothing stood before us. "Oh," he said in surprise, and seemed almost a little disappointed. "Oh, it's kids."

"Sir Thomas London," began Lilli.

"Is it Halloween already?" asked the old man.

Lilli was puzzled. "What?"

"I don't have anything sweet to give you," London stammered.

"It's about a treasure. The treasure of Lotterlulu!"

Suddenly the old fellow came to life. His eyes sparkled, he stood up straighter; he looked like a new man. "Ha! Why didn't you say so in the first place? In with you, you little rascals!" He closed the door behind us and rubbed his hands. "What can I get you? Coke, coffee or something stronger?" He gave a strange laugh.

"Chips would be great," Marvin cried out enthusiastically.

"We need your help to dig up Lotterlulu's treasure," Lilli said.

"You know where it is? Then you're a step ahead of me." Sir London bent down and looked Lilli in the eye, long and hard. "Where?" he suddenly burst out.

"It's...it's in the lake," said Lilli, taken aback.

Sir London straightened up again and seemed disappointed. His shoulders sagged, his eyes looked tired. The old fellow hobbled over to the table with the help of his walking stick and fell into a chair. "No, it's not there."

"That's the only possibility," Lilli continued. "The ship was suddenly gone, the river was blockaded and there was only one canal leading to the lake."

"You've put the pieces together nicely, little lady. But I thought of that already. I've had sonar imaging done of the bottom of the lake. There's nothing there but sludge."

"That's impossible!" protested Lilli.

"The images are on the desk over there. See for yourself."

Marvin and I went over to the table. A jumble of photos, scraps of paper and old things lay on top of it. All clues Sir London had collected during his search for Lotterlulu's treasure.

"He's right, Lilli," I said. "Here are the photos, you can't see anything on them."

"Okay, and if that's all you have, I'm afraid I can't help you any further."

Lilli looked at him in desperation. "No, you have to help us. We have to find the treasure. And it has to be today, or my grandpa will lose his house. You know my grandpa. He helped you too. He let you take photos of Lotterlulu's portrait."

"That was your grandpa? What a small world," London murmured.

"I don't believe it. That's..." I'd noticed something, and I stared at the treasure hunter in astonishment. First I took a moment to let my gaze sweep the hotel room. It was large and equipped with lots of amenities. But the treasure hunter's personal possessions were particularly interesting. Over there was an easel and paint. Then a huge suitcase, a bird cage, a large pile of books, a camera and much more.

"You're going to help us," I said in a firm voice. "Because if you don't, we'll report you to the police for theft!"

"What?" Sir London looked at me, dumbfounded. "Where did you get the idea I'd stolen something?"

"Well," I said, "the evidence is right here on your table."

 How did I realize Sir London was most likely a thief?

CHAPTER 11

The Theft

"YOU HEARD RIGHT. YOU stole the portrait of Lotterlulu from Lilli's grandpa," I declared.

Lilli and Marvin stared at me in disbelief. If it turned out to be untrue, then I was screwing up our only chance of getting professional help from the treasure hunter. But I was certain.

"That's quite an accusation, young man," Sir London said. "But it's also utter nonsense. As Lilli rightly pointed out, her grandfather let me take photos of the portrait in great detail. It would have been pointless to steal it once I had them. Besides, I never had the opportunity to anyway."

"I don't know why you wanted the original either, maybe there's something on the back of it. And I'm sure you had the chance – Lilli's grandpa made you coffee. He had to go into the kitchen to do that, leaving you alone with the painting."

Lilli looked at me in shock. "Timmi, the painting was still there when we left!"

"It's a fake," I retorted. "Here's what happened. Yesterday Sir London went and took detailed photos of the painting. Then he came back to his hotel room and painted a copy of the portrait as best he could. On the easel over there. That's why he went to see your grandpa again this morning and claimed that a few photos hadn't turned out. When your grandpa made coffee, he quickly swapped the original for the copy."

Sir London's laughter rang through the room. "Nice story. And Lilli's grandfather can't even tell the difference between the original and a counterfeit? He has owned the painting for decades; he knows it inside and out."

"Firstly, Lilli's grandpa is old and doesn't see well anymore. Secondly...I can prove it!" I went over to the table with the sonar images of the lake and the other clues to the whereabouts of Lotterlulu's treasure.

"Right on top here is one of the photos you took yesterday. It's clearly marked with yesterday's date. Down here is one of the photos you took this morning. Also dated. If you compare the photos, you can see that the picture frame was hanging the other way up yesterday. After you were there it was upside down. You swapped the painting and in your hurry to be done you put the forged painting in the frame the wrong way up."

"No!" Marvin said, flabbergasted.

You could see Lilli was getting mad again.

"And by the way, you also painted an extra earring", I added and gave Sir London a challenging stare. He had that sparkle in his eye again. Suddenly he stood, looking years younger again, and headed straight over to us to take a good look at the photos himself.

"Interesting, very interesting," he murmured, "but there's still a little piece of the puzzle missing. Lilli's grandfather will confirm that the only thing I had on me was my camera. How in the world do you think I could have smuggled the forgery in and the original back out? It's not like I could have folded it up and put it in my pants pocket, is it? It would have gotten all creased."

"I know, I know!" Marvin cheered. We all turned to look at him. Marvin put his feet together and stood up straight. Then he held up the forefinger of his right hand and continued. "You didn't only have your camera on you. I'm sure of it. And the other thing you had enabled you to smuggle the paintings in and out right under Lilli's grandpa's nose. It's such an inconspicuous thing, no-one would notice it. It's right here in this room. Who can see it, who can see it?" Marvin jumped up and down on the spot excitedly.

 Which inconspicuous object could Sir London have used to smuggle the portrait out?

CHAPTER 12

The Lost Symbol

OF COURSE! IT HAD to be the walking stick. Sir London wouldn't have left the house without his walking stick. Marvin was already screwing the handle off it, while Sir London grinned and nodded appreciatively. He didn't seem to mind, in fact he seemed to be pleased about how perceptive we were. There was a 'pop' and the stick separated into two pieces in Marvin's hands.

"Hah!" said Marvin, "I knew it." He held the hollow walking stick at an angle so we could see inside.

Lilli was mad as a hornet. "Come on, we're going!" she growled and stomped toward the door.

"Wait, not so fast," Sir London exclaimed. "You've already proven you're real little detectives. If you want, I'll tell you what I've put together about the treasure so far. As a kind of reward."

"That's not enough! From now on we're partners," I said and pulled out my asthma puffer. My own courage was cutting off my air supply. After I'd inhaled the spray, I continued. "We need your help. You know all about treasures. And you need some strong legs. Plus, many hands make light work, as my mom always says."

He eyed me carefully. Maybe he suspected he really didn't have a choice.

"Okay, agreed. You've got yourselves a partner," Sir London laughed. "But don't get your hopes up. So far I'm as much in the dark as you are." He shuffled over to his chair, grabbed the pieces of his walking stick out of Marvin's hands and began to screw it back together. "I only know this much. The pirate Lotterlulu was stinking rich. He knew he was being hunted and he planned his escape in advance. Him turning up here and the disappearance of his ship – it was no coincidence, it was all planned down to the last detail."

◈ ◈ ◈

We crowded around him as he told us about Lotterlulu's raids. Every so often we got up and looked at the maps that were lying around, the drawings and photos of old pirate ships, buildings, people and places. Lilli calmed down and listened attentively. Marvin sat there captivated. Most of the time his jaw hung limp, leaving his mouth hanging open.

"When Lotterlulu finally got too rich, so rich that even his old friends were about ready to come after him, he decided to end his pirating career and go into hiding. I firmly believe the disappearance of the Star Runner had to be organized well in advance. That's why I started looking into it, and I think Lotterlulu arrived here quite a while before his ship did. Disguised as a rich nobleman under a false name."

"Whatever he did here, he made sure there was no record of it. And with such a lot of money, he must have been able to make extensive preparations for the arrival of the Star Runner and for its disappearance. All I know about is his charitable works, though. For example, he gave large sums to the local parish. He had his finger in many pies, but I can't find a single clue as to what exactly he was up to."

Lilli leaned over the old maps, paintings and drawings. Something had captured her attention. She went over to the other table, picked up a photo of the portrait of Lotterlulu and went back to the first desk. She seemed to be comparing the portrait with something on the desk. "I think I've found something," she said excitedly. "Look, see how they match? That's where we have to go!"

What did Lilli mean when she said "they match"?

- Academy of Arts
- City Well
- Southern Market Place
- Free Church St. Marina
- Bath House
- City Theater
- Court of Justice
- Town Hall
- City Library
- Hospital
- Academy of Science
- Chamber of Crafts
- Chamber of Commerce
- Southern City Gate
- Northern City Gate
- West City Gate
- City Harbor
- Shipyard
- River Tower West
- River Tower East
- Fishers Market Hall
- City Watch South
- Jail
- Park of Roses
- Astronomers Observatory
- St. Jonah Elijah Church
- St. Nici Church
- Cathedral
- Little Church
- Old Church
- Main Market
- Lake Watergate
- River Watergate
- Lake Harbor
- Monument of P...
- Monument of ...
- Place of Triun...
- Bridge of Cra...
- Bridge of Sh...
- Bridge of Se...
- Bridge of V...
- Bridge of ...

The Star Runner

IT WAS TRUE! THE symbol on the pirate's necklace could also be seen on the legend of the map: a star and a half moon. The exact same one. That couldn't be a coincidence. We had another hot lead and every one of us could feel it.

"Which church is that?" Marvin asked, eyes shining.

"That, my little partner, is the Free Church of St. Marina. It's dedicated to seafarers and its construction was completed in the year the Star Runner disappeared!"

Sir London's voice sounded full and strong, and when I looked at him he was standing tall, both hands on his hips, chest sticking out in determination. This man didn't need a walking stick today. "Pack up your things, gather your courage and your thirst for adventure. We're off to St. Marina!" he declared.

Marvin looked around at all of us, his eyes wide with joy, and began to jump up and down on the spot again, clapping his hands wildly.

❖ ❖ ❖

When we reached St. Marina it was already afternoon. The heat lay heavy over the houses. The sun, which was already low in the sky, immersed the church in a promising light. You could see the unmistakable marks time had left on the building, which was rather small for a house of God. It looked old and gray, and kind of forsaken. Slowly we climbed the few steps to the entrance and hoped like heck it would be open.

When the cool air inside the church hit our faces we were relieved.

"It's open, it's open!" whispered Marvin, obviously thrilled.

The door fell shut behind us and we scanned the room.

"Clearly for seafarers," Lilli marveled.

Objects from the sea world decorated the walls as far as the eye could see. There were maps of the ocean, model ships, ropes with all different kinds of knots, a ship's wheel, fishing nets and much more.

"You would have thought they'd build a church like this by water," Lilli said.

Sir London stared at Lilli, a blank expression on his face. Suddenly, as if he'd been stung by a bee, he began to rummage around in his briefcase, pulling out a folded up piece of paper. He knelt down and spread the map out on the cold stone floor. It showed the town center in the time of Lotterlulu. "Ha! You're right. Very good, Lilli." He looked pleased. "The church is by water! The old canal joining the river and the lake runs behind the church."

"Um, guys?" I whispered and took a few steps to the side as I looked towards the end of the church. "Don't you notice anything funny? The columns are right in the middle of the aisle and back there, the platform where the pastor gives his sermons – it's really high, there's a staircase leading up to it."

Lilli followed my gaze, but couldn't make out what I saw. "So what? What is it, Timmi?"

"Well, the walls are curved and the chandeliers on the ceiling are held up with ropes."

Marvin stared at me in astonishment. "It looks like a ship! As if the church itself was a ship."

Now they all saw it. The columns in the aisle were the masts of the ship, the platform with the altar was the helm and the walls of the church were gently curved as if following the outline of a boat.

"Amazing," murmured Sir London. "They built the church like a ship."

"No, no," I said. "They didn't build it *like* a ship. They built it *around* the ship." I could barely believe it myself as I said it:

"May I present, the Star Runner!"

It was almost too unbelievable to be true. We ran excitedly through the church, and everything seemed to fit.

"Look!" Marvin called down from the helm. He took the ship's wheel from where it hung decoratively on the wall and carried it to the place on the helm where it probably once belonged, letting it slip into the mounting there. It snapped cleanly into place, where Marvin turned it gently left and right.

What we couldn't find, though, was access to the ship's hold.

❖ ❖ ❖

After we'd searched fruitlessly for a while, I came across Sir London, who was standing in front of the ship's wheel, lost in thought.

"Look," he said when he noticed me. "There are numbers all around the wheel. When I turn it, I hear a click every time one of the numbers passes the highest point."

"Like on a safe."

"Exactly! Tell the others we're looking for a numerical code. Normally it would be three numbers between one and twelve. I bet the code is hidden here somewhere. The numbers might be represented by other objects. Imagine different candle holders for example. In one of them there are five candles, in another three and in the last one four. Do you get what I mean?"

"I get it."

"Good, then let's get to it."

"Sir London?"

"What is it?"

"I think I already know the three numbers."

"Come again?"

What were the three numbers?

CHAPTER 14

One Man Alone

THERE WERE SOME SPOKES missing on the ship's wheel itself, in fact exactly by the numbers one, three and five. We may not have known the correct sequence, but Sir London got it first try (it was one, five and then three). A loud, dull clunk resonated through the church after he turned the wheel three times, each time so that one of the numbers was right at the top. The clunk sounded as if someone had opened a big vacuum sealed jar of grape jelly.

"What was that?" I asked.

"Whatever it was, it's a good sign. We're on the right track," Sir London said.

From the edge of the helm we had a good view of the rest of the ship. We searched hard for the source of the sound.

"There!" cried Lilli and pointed to the middle of the church. A fair bit of dust swirled like mad in a wide ray of light. "Something moved over there."

"Quick," said Marvin.

We darted over, full of excitement. This was the big moment. We had really discovered something! Maybe it was the treasure.

"Whatever you do, don't touch anything," called Sir London, who couldn't keep up.

It was just as we'd hoped. A secret door. A stone floor plate about 3 feet long and wide had popped out, although only by a few inches, so that the entrance it hid remained closed off. It looked heavy. There was painting on its surface, which was continued on the neighboring plates, causing the secret door to blend in with its surroundings.

When Sir London joined us he smiled, then wrinkled his forehead. "A tile as a door. Probably with a hinge on one side. It looks heavy. Let's try lifting it."

We positioned ourselves so that each of us could get a good grip on one part of it. Even Sir London joined in.

"Ready? On three. One, two, three!" he yelled and we pulled with all our might.

It didn't move an inch. We slid to the ground, exhausted, and stared at the stubborn plate.

"What now?" asked Marvin.

Sir London examined the small crack between the floor and the secret door. "The tile seems to be really massive. Even with a crowbar we wouldn't be able to do anything with it. Strange."

"Strange?" I asked. "Why is that strange?"

"Surely Lotterlulu wouldn't have let many people in on the secret of the treasure. I would have thought he'd have installed a mechanism here to allow him to get to it alone. But no-one on earth could get this tile up without help. You can't even really get a good grip on it. You'd need something to pull it up with."

"Like a handle?" Lilli asked, and looked at the painting covering the plate.

I immediately saw what she meant. A large cast-iron ring was painted on it. "What if that's not just decorative?" I murmured excitedly.

Lilli jumped up, grabbed a chair and smashed its leg into the picture. After only one blow, stone crumbled away from the tile and a small hole became visible.

"Unbelievable," said Sir London. "There's a real handle under the painted one."

After a few minutes the massive ring was revealed. But even with the help of this handhold, we couldn't lift the plate up any further.

"We need something really heavy we can tie to the ring. Something that can lift the tile for us," I said and looked around.

"Yes," Sir London agreed. "Lotterlulu will certainly have built something into the church that could help him open the secret door alone. Look around, see if you can find what it was."

 Can you tell how the secret entrance could have been opened?

CHAPTER 15

Trapped

IT WAS PRETTY STRANGE that the heavy chandelier above us was tied to two ship's ropes but only one of them was holding its weight. We took the loose one, unwound it from the pillar it was wrapped around and Sir London tied it to the ring on the floor tile with a sailor's knot. Now we only needed to cut the rope holding up the chandelier with one of the swords or sabers hanging on the church wall, and the chandelier would come crashing down, pulling the tile up.

Sir London grasped the sword with both hands and positioned himself next to the rope that needed cutting. "Get back, kids. Behind the column. If this goes wrong, there could be all sorts of bits and pieces flying around like shrapnel."

He lifted the sword over his head with both hands and we started to run away. "Take cover!" Sir London called out and gave the rope a mighty chop.

Huddled behind one of the columns, we heard more hacking.

"Now," Sir London yelled and gave one last, powerful blow. For what seemed like an eternity, we heard nothing. Then came a loud crashing and clattering which soon seemed to echo from every direction. After a few seconds, absolute silence set in. We hesitantly stepped out from behind the column. First we saw Sir London, lying on the ground. He had probably saved himself with a head-long dive out of the danger zone. Impressive for an old man.

But he seemed to be okay, because he was grinning as he looked over at the floor tile. Then we saw it. The heavy chandelier was swinging back and forth on the rope tied to the tile, which creaked under the strain. The floor tile now stood wide open, leaving behind a gaping black hole. My heart was beating like crazy and Marvin started jumping up and down again, clapping his hands.

"We did it," whispered Lilli.

A glance inside the hole revealed a wooden ladder which led down into darkness. "We need a flashlight," I said.

Marvin seemed to have spotted something, and reached into the hole. "Look, Lotterlulu thought of everything." He pulled out an old oil lamp, which had been attached to the ceiling of the room below us.

A few minutes later we were climbing carefully down the rickety ladder by the light of the old oil lamp. Sir London went first, holding the lamp out ahead of him. Before each step he checked with a few stomps to see that the rungs would still hold. Once there was a terrible crack as one of them gave way and fell to pieces. It smelled musty; the air was damp and incredibly stuffy.

Sir London said, "There's not a lot of oxygen in here, we better hurry."

Arriving at the bottom, Sir London held the lamp up high and we gave our eyes a bit of time to adjust to the dim light. Everything around us seemed to be made of wood. We were clearly in the hull of a ship.

"It really is the Star Runner," Sir London said, thinking out loud. "I'm gradually starting to understand how his escape must have gone."

Suddenly, we heard a loud thud followed by a far off sounding clatter. The floor tile! We looked up in horror.

"It's fallen shut," cried Lilli.

"This...this can't be," stammered Sir London.

I quickly climbed the ladder and pushed against the tile with all my might. "No way that's moving," I said, and panic crept over me. Still clinging to the ladder, I reached for my inhaler.

For a few seconds it was dead silent. Then Sir London seemed to make up his mind. "We have to get out of here. Now. The oxygen won't last much longer. We're going to search the hull now, maybe we'll find another way out or something that can help us get the tile off. I want to hear every idea, no matter how crazy. Get to work!"

We were about to jump to it and start searching the cupboards, compartments and chests, when Lilli shouted "Stop! Don't move!"

We all froze.

"What is it? What is it?" I groaned, having just picked up a heavy cannon ball.

 What hazard had Lilli discovered?

CHAPTER 16

A Pirate's Realm

IF SIR LONDON HAD opened the door, the hidden wire would have set off the pirate's rifle in the cupboard. Lilli had just saved Sir London's life. Even though the gun was from Lotterlulu's time, it might still have fired. We cut the wire and left the gun untouched.

Lilli elbowed Sir London, gave him a cheeky look and whispered, "You owe me one."

By the light of the oil lamp, we crept step by step, ever deeper into the ship's damp, dark hull. Everything appeared to have been left unchanged. You might easily have thought the ship was still anchored in a harbor and we had travelled back in time. As if we had stowed away on board and could be discovered at any moment by the crew or captain Lotterlulu. Slowly we made our way towards the back end of the ship.

First we came across a series of smaller rooms with double beds. How I wished we had the time to rummage through the belongings left behind there. But we had to be quick. We were shut in and needed to find a way out. Or something that could create a way out for us. In the very first cabin I found it: dynamite.

Lilli looked worried. "Will it even ignite? After all these years?"

Sir London held a stick up close to the light of the lamp. "Oh yes, it will. Pirate ships were always damp, so special measures were taken to protect the fuse and powder." His face creased in a frown. "But I'm not sure whether we'll be able to blow the tile open with it. The pressure of the explosion would mostly be directed down into the hull. Let's keep looking."

With every step, the wooden beams creaked beneath our feet. Most of the time we couldn't see more than a few feet by the light of the oil lamp. Again and again, eerie shapes appeared in the darkness at the end of the corridors. We were all scared stiff. Only hectically searching all the rooms and chests took our minds off the spooky surroundings.

A few minutes later we ended up standing in front of a large leather-paneled door. "The captain's cabin," I whispered in awe.

Sir London nodded at me in silence. This was where Lotterlulu had lived. His own private realm. Trembling, I gripped the cold door handle. The hinges creaked terribly as the large room opened up before us, and we saw something none of us had been expecting: light!

On the opposite wall was a big, round window with thick glass. A porthole. A dim, bluish light streamed in through it. Marvin was the first to approach the porthole. "Is it a way out?" He looked into the light, trying to make out what was on the other side of the glass. "What is that?"

"Water," said Sir London dryly. "We're underground, and that there...that's the canal that leads from the river to the lake. Now I know how he was able to make the Star Runner disappear. Lotterlulu arrived here before the ship did and promised to fund the construction of a church for seafarers. As compensation, this was to be the last port-of-call for his ship. He probably first had them erect a hall, and then got them to dig out a deep cavity inside it. The hall with its cavity was built right beside the canal."

"And in that way, he was able to secretly let water into the hole," Marvin whispered, fascinated.

"Exactly. On a foggy night, the ship left the harbor and followed the canal all the way along to this spot. Here, everything was ready for it. The side of the hall facing the canal was a kind of gate you could open and close. The Star Runner got parked in here like a car in a garage, without any chance of being discovered."

"And the church was built around it," Lilli concluded. "Since then, no-one has ever set foot in here again."

"No, that's not quite right," said Sir London. "There has definitely been someone else in here. I'm not sure when, but certainly after Lotterlulu."

"I know what you mean," added Marvin.

How did Sir London know someone had been in the cabin since Lotterlulu?

CHAPTER 17

The Plan

IN AMONGST SOME OTHER bottles, a Coke bottle was to be seen, which was definitely not as old as the rest of the ship.

"It's true that Coke has been around since the end of the eighteenth century, but that was well after Lotterlulu's time," explained Sir London.

"It wouldn't have expired until next year," whispered Marvin, looking at the bottle.

Lilli lowered her voice too, as if someone else might have been down there with us. "If someone was here recently, why didn't they tell anyone about their find?"

For a few chilling moments, no-one said anything.

"Oh, never mind, how do we get out of here?" asked Lilli.

Sir London's face was lit up by the blue light as he stared into it. "We swim!"

"What?" I cried.

"We blast a hole in the wall, right here," he continued, determined.

"But...but..." Lilli stammered.

"Trust me," Sir London said, meeting our questioning expressions with an insistent look. "Search the ship for something to protect us from the explosion. It has to be big enough for all of us, and very sturdy."

❖ ❖ ❖

The plan to blow a hole in the wall, leading right into the canal, seemed more than risky. Even if we managed to stay safe from the explosion, we still wouldn't have gotten anywhere, because a deluge of water would follow. While Lilli and Marvin began to search right away, I couldn't keep from sharing my concerns with Sir London. He knelt down beside me.

"Timmi, right now our concern is the air. We're running out of oxygen," he explained calmly. "When we light the dynamite, the explosion becomes our problem. After that, the power of the incoming water. And finally the way through the water, out of here. We might have to dive quite far. And in the dark, no less, since the lamp won't work underwater. That's going to be our last task."

My throat tightened just thinking of it.

"This is an important life lesson. If you try to solve all your problems at once, you'll be overwhelmed. But if you deal with them one after the other, you've got a good chance of getting through. And that's exactly what we're going to do now, okay?" He stood, held the lamp up high and turned to Lilli and Marvin. "There's nothing here. Let's search the rest of the ship."

❖ ❖ ❖

I stood there a moment, dazed. When I emerged from my state of shock shortly afterward, the others had already gone on ahead. The light of the lamp flickered occasionally in the darkness beyond the captain's cabin. I was alone in the room full of blue light. Once again, I took a puff of my inhaler.

A large, solid wooden table covered with all kinds of documents, nautical charts and measuring instruments stood in a corner of the captain's cabin. By one wall there was a shelf full of old books. Right next to it was a bed. But what grabbed my attention most was the little desk to the right of the porthole.

All sorts of papers lay scattered across it too. In the darkness, I could barely decipher them, but I thought they were drawings and the construction plans of the church. There also seemed to be a map of the city, with a bundle of letters next to it. I decided to stuff as many of the papers into my pockets as I could. Then I noticed it. Hanging on the wall above the desk was a kind of granite slab with a mysterious phrase on it. Some of the words seemed oddly familiar.

"Timmi!" came a voice from somewhere in the distance.

"Coming!" I cast one last glance at the text, trying to memorize it. Then I began to feel my way through the darkness towards the voices and the oil lamp, whose light flared up every so often.

Moments later I found myself with the others in a large storeroom.

"We've got it!" Marvin cheered and pointed to an old cast-iron bathtub.

"That?" I asked.

"Exactly," said Sir London. He was all excited and gestured wildly as he spoke. "We'll tip it on its side, lean it against the wall and hide behind it. It will protect us from the explosion and also from the first big blast of water."

"Water?" squeaked Lilli.

"Yes, exactly. Once there's enough water in here that the in-ward current eases off, we'll have to cover about 30 yards to get to the hole. Depending on how quickly the water rises, we might have to swim or dive," Sir London clarified.

"Dive?" Lilli gulped.

"In total darkness, since the oil lamp will have gone out."

As if that wasn't enough, I suddenly smelled something burn. I glanced over to the oil lamp and spotted a trail of smoldering black powder.

"Watch out," I yelled. "Quick!"

Everyone looked at me in horror.

 What gave me such a fright?

The Darkness

SIR LONDON REACTED QUICK as a flash and pulled the fuse from the cannon. It turned out that the cannon wasn't loaded, but we had gotten quite a shock all the same. A short while later, Sir London attached a long rope to the wall next to the tub in the storeroom with an expert sailor's knot. He planned to run the rope all the way to the captain's cabin, so that after the explosion we could pull ourselves along it from the protective tub all the way to the freshly made hole. Otherwise we'd never find our way in the pitch black with the water rushing in at us.

Lilli examined the knot with a critical eye. "Hopefully this one holds."

"Don't tell me you think my knot came undone and let the tile fall down!" Sir London replied indignantly.

"Well, a thick rope like that can't have snapped," Lilli grumbled.

"There is a third possibility," Sir London said in a low voice, more to himself than to anyone else.

We began to drag the rope towards the captain's cabin, pulling it tight and fixing it to the wall every few yards.

"And what would that be? It was either the knot or the rope, I can't think of anything else it could have been," Lilli insisted.

"Then let's leave it at that for now," groaned Sir London. He was breathing hard. It wasn't just pulling the rope that was getting to him, but the thin air too.

"We're getting short on oxygen," Sir London gasped. "We have to hurry."

"What's the other possibility?" Lilli wasn't giving up.

Sir London seemed to realize she'd be like a dog with a bone until he told her. "It's probably nothing more than a myth."

Marvin's ears pricked up at that. "A myth?"

Quietly and calmly, Sir London went on. "There are many rumors about Lotterlulu's last raid. He's supposed to have stolen a legendary object. The myth told of the object being protected by a mysterious 'Dark Power' which would find it anywhere. According to legend, the people in service of this Dark Power, the so-called Guardians, only have black nothingness where their eyes and mouths should be. Don't worry, that part's just nonsense. But when Lotterlulu realized how hopeless his situation was, he aligned himself with these Guardians and created a hiding place for the object that was better than any of his previous hiding places. He left the object there and disappeared forever."

Marvin jumped up and down in excitement. "What was the object?"

Lilli asked quietly, "You think someone from that Dark Power cut the rope? And maybe it was one of those Guardians that left the Coke bottle here too?"

Only then did I notice we'd already arrived at the captain's cabin.

Sir London held the oil lamp in front of our faces and gave us a meaningful look. "I'll tell you more once we're out of here. Look alive."

Suddenly the lamp went out. Even the light from the porthole seemed to have dimmed and was barely perceptible anymore. The sun must have been low in the sky by then.

Sir London gave the lamp a good shake. "I need light to tie the sailor's knot."

"Oh come on Sir, you can do it, even in the dark," I tried to encourage him.

"Absolutely not," he said helplessly. "And we've only got one match."

"We need it for the dynamite," said Lilli. Her voice came out of the darkness, somewhere to my right. Only now did I realize we really could barely see our hands in front of our faces. It seemed to be getting darker by the second.

"No-one touches the match. Not even to light a candle or a lamp. Because if it doesn't work, we've got no match left to light the dynamite," Sir London said. "And now think! Where can we find some light in this infernal darkness?"

In my mind's eye, I pictured the room and the objects lying around in it...

 How could we light up the room without matches?

CHAPTER 19

Running Out of Steam

I TOOK ONE PHOTO after another, using the flash from Sir London's camera to allow him to see momentarily. He tied the rope in a complicated sailor's knot and wedged the stick of dynamite right next to the porthole. Everything was ready.

"Okay kids, get back and hide behind the tub while I light the fuse," Sir London said.

"You're not really quick on foot. You might not make it back to the tub in time," I pointed out.

Lilli agreed. "And without you, we won't be able to move the tub."

Sir London thought it over in silence a while, grumbling every now and then. Although I couldn't make it out in the darkness, I felt his gaze gradually settle on me.

"Timmi, you're the fastest of us all. You're going to have to light the fuse, do you think you can do it?" asked Sir London.

My heart sank. I'd been able to suppress my fear this whole time, but now it hit me with full force. Sometimes I had nightmares which I thought were real while I was dreaming, and when I woke up I was infinitely happy they hadn't been real after all. That was what I wanted right now – to wake up. "Of course I can do it," I heard myself say.

❖ ❖ ❖

A short time later I was left alone in the darkness of the captain's cabin. Sir London guessed the fuse would burn for ten to twenty seconds before the explosion. That's how much time I'd have to get back to the others behind the tub, without being able to see anything. In my mind's eye I once again pictured the route I'd soon have to run back.

"Okay Timmi, now!" a voice rang out from the back of the ship. They were ready. I had to light it.

Trembling, I pressed our only match to the matchbox. This had to work. Determined, I dragged the matchhead along the side and was rewarded with a bright flame, which jumped utterly unexpectedly straight across to the fuse. The fuse was burning! Horrified, I saw how quickly the flame was eating its way towards the dynamite. Far too rapid.

I turned on the spot and ran as fast as I could out of the cabin, then left, then right and then, followed by a dull thud, straight into a wall. My head was ringing and I lay flat on the floor. All around me was absolute darkness. I felt for the rope and found it.

"Timmi!" I heard from somewhere in the distance. Then came the explosion. It was deafening. The water followed immediately. I felt as if I was hanging on to a rope in the middle of a waterfall.

I quickly found myself completely submerged. Things whirled around in the current and banged into me painfully. It was insanely cold. I clung to the rope for dear life. I felt the undertow gradually lessen, then I ran out of air. I let go of the rope and pushed upwards. I could breathe! The water didn't go right up to the ceiling. It had formed an air pocket.

Soon afterwards, the others joined me. We each took a deep breath, dove under and swam from the flooded Star Runner. When we finally emerged from the ship, we found ourselves swimming in the canal and felt as if reborn. We yelled and cheered like crazy. But then our moods suddenly changed.

"How are we going to get out of here?" asked Lilli.

The walls of the canal were slippery and there wasn't a ladder or anything similar in sight. We heard voices above us. It was a market. You could see a melon stand.

"Hello, can anybody help us?" For a few minutes we screamed our throats raw.

"They can't hear us," I said, exhausted. "It's too noisy up there in the marketplace."

"We better think of something fast," said Sir London in a gloomy voice. "I'm afraid I can't cope much longer." He once again looked like the old man that he was. We didn't have much time.

"We need some way to get up there," said Lilli.

"Wait, I think I saw something in the Star Runner," I called out and dove back under. *We've got a fully equipped pirate ship here,* I thought as I swam back through the hole and inside the captain's cabin.

What was I hoping to use to climb the wall?

CHAPTER 20

Under Observation

BULLSEYE! THE GRAPPLING HOOK caught on the melon net and a flood of the big fruits came tumbling into the water. The owner of the melon stand and lots of other people from the market immediately rushed over and stood by the railing staring down at us, stunned. We each grabbed onto one of the floating melons and waved happily up at them. We were saved!

❖ ❖ ❖

We spent the rest of the evening with our parents at the hospital and the police station. It seemed to take forever before I was finally able to sit in my room, undisturbed, and think back on all we'd been through. I opened the window, sat on the sill and looked up at the stars. A warm evening breeze was blowing.

"What an adventure," I murmured to myself. Images from the day shot through my head willy-nilly. So much had happened. We'd been incredibly lucky. And still so much was left unsolved. What was this 'Dark Power' Sir London had mentioned? Had someone cut the rope in the church to trap us inside? And most of all – why wasn't there any treasure in the Star Runner's hull?

Without the treasure it really had all been for nothing. Lilli's grandpa would be thrown out of his house tomorrow morning. Of course, he never would have wanted us to risk our lives to help him, but we couldn't have known it would end up like that. Now we'd had quite the adventure, but hadn't reached our goal.

If only we'd had more time to search the Star Runner, maybe we would have found a clue. The sheets of paper I'd taken with me had been completely ruined by the water. The only thing I could remember that might hold a clue as to the whereabouts of the treasure, was the strange writing next to the porthole. But no matter how hard I tried, I couldn't recall the text.

Suddenly it dawned on me. I sat bolt upright on the windowsill. If I was right, then all was not lost yet. Feeling guilty towards my parents, I quickly shoved a few things into my backpack, slipped into some clothes and my trainers, and snuck out of the house.

❖ ❖ ❖

Lilli and Marvin were game too, although it wasn't easy to lure them to their windows to let them in on my plan. About an hour later we approached the Hotel Savoy, which was radiant with its many lights. This time there was no bellhop at the door. We decided to hide nearby and wait for some guests to approach. When they opened the door, we would slip in with them.

After observing the entrance for a couple of minutes, Marvin narrowed his eyes and whispered, "Am I crazy or is the hotel being watched?"

"You are crazy, no matter what", said Lilli.

I tried to follow his gaze but couldn't make out what he had spotted. "Are you sure?" I asked.

Marvin turned back to Lilli and me. "Don't know if it has to do with Sir London or us at all, but the entrance is being watched. Has been for at least an hour now I'd guess."

How could Marvin tell someone must have been watching the hotel for some time already?

CHAPTER 21

The Treasure Map

A FEW MOMENTS LATER we had successfully managed to sneak into the Savoy. "There, the car. See all the cigarettes?" asked Marvin as he pointed it out.

Sir London had to press his face right up against the window to see the car from his hotel room. It must have looked pretty silly from down below. "Yes, I see it," Sir London grumbled. "Those are cigarillos. Judging by that pile of them, they must have been there for quite some time already. Strange, you can't make out the smokers face. Must be too dark outside."

"Who is it?" asked Lilli.

Frowning, Sir London turned to us. "Maybe no-one." He reached for the phone and, without asking us, ordered three cups of hot cocoa. "Room service will bring you up something warm in a minute."

Lilli crossed her arms and asked a bit more insistently, "And who do you think they are?"

"Maybe it's the Guardians of the secret we were searching for."

"*Are* searching for, we *are* still searching for it!" said Lilli.

I nodded and whispered, "The followers of the Dark Power. No eyes and no mouth."

"I don't know much about this secret society," Sir London went on, "but Lotterlulu must have been very afraid of them. After joining their society, he used his riches to build a well-protected hiding place for the object they guard. Better than any other hiding place he had ever set up before. Even better than that of the Star Runner."

"That was hundreds of years ago," I pointed out.

Sir London nodded. "It would be amazing if there really were still Guardians nowadays. On the other hand..." He seemed to be wondering whether to go on or not, but then he did. "After our swimming trip I went up into the church again."

I knew right away why. He had taken a look at the rope that had held open the tile so we could enter the hull of the Star Runner.

"Had it torn or was it cut?" I asked excitedly.

"The rope...was cut," Sir London said with raised eyebrows.

Marvin went white. "Someone wanted to trap us in there."

"We have to tread carefully," Sir London agreed.

Lilli looked at me. "And we have to hurry."

Right, I thought to myself and turned to Sir London. "We need the film from the camera."

❖ ❖ ❖

Steaming hot cocoa stood before us minutes later, as we examined the little negatives from the camera by the light of a lamp. You could hardly see anything. One by one, we searched the pictures for the phrase on the wall in the captain's cabin.

"There it is!" I called out. "Quick, get a magnifying glass." It was a slam dunk. The writing was clear and legible.

"From triumph to liberty. From justice to peace," murmured Sir London.

"What can that mean?" Lilli whispered. "And aren't those the names of places on the old city map?"

"It's a clue to the whereabouts of the treasure," said Marvin.

"I think so too," Sir London agreed.

Marvin looked at him in surprise. "Really?"

"Get the map." We spread it out before him. "What is that clue trying to tell us? Maybe it points to a certain location," Sir London wondered.

 What place was the riddle pointing to?

Academy of Arts
City Well
Southern Market Place
Free Church St. Marina
Birth House
City Theater
Court of Justice
Town Hall
City Library
Hospital
Academy of Science
Chamber of Crafts
Chamber of Commerce
Southern City Gate
Northern City Gate
West City Gate
City Ha...
Shipyard
River Tow...
P...
Fishers Market H...
C...
Park of Roses
Astronomers Observatory
St. Jacobs Church
St. Nui Church
Cathedral
Little Church
Old Church
Main Market
Lake Watergate
River Watergate
Lake Harbor
Monument of Peace
Monument of Freedom
Place of Triumph
Bridge of Crabs
Bridge of Shells

From Triumph
to Freedom.
From Justice
to Peace.

CHAPTER 22

Under Your Feet

TO BE ON THE safe side we had left the Savoy by its rear entrance and a little while later found ourselves in the market place. Back at the hotel, we had drawn a line between the symbols marking the Monument of Freedom and the Place of Triumph as well as another line between the Court of Justice and the Monument of Peace. The main market lay right at their intersection.

The clouds above us moved unusually fast and whenever they left the moon enough room, it would illuminate the surroundings with its pale light. An eerie silence prevailed.

"Where should we start?" whispered Marvin.

Lilli turned in a circle and looked around. "There's nothing here."

Sir London scrutinized the floor. "The hiding place will probably be underground. We're looking for the entrance. Maybe we'll find a symbol on one of the paving tiles."

While the others started searching tile by tile, my gaze wandered to the edge of the area where I saw a digger and all kinds of construction equipment. Next to that was a pallet of paving stones. I walked slowly over to it. My head swam and I hoped I was wrong. When I took a look at the pavers up close and then turned back to the market place, I knew it. We had a problem.

❖ ❖ ❖

"Um, guys?" I called out. "They've redone it all." The others looked at me in disbelief.

Sir London kneeled down and ran his hands over one of the paving stones. "This can't be."

Lilli rushed over to me as if she wanted to check the pavers in the pallet herself. "Oh no!"

But Marvin seemed to have found something else. He stood in front of an information box, which was poorly lit up by a flickering neon light.

"Come on," I said to Lilli. We hurried over and crowded together around the display.

"Here's a description of the work they're doing," said Marvin. You could see before and after pictures of the market place.

Sir London pointed to a marker in the before picture. "Look, there was an entrance to the old sewer system. It says it hadn't been used for a long time, so they closed it off as part of the re-vamp." He paused for a moment to think. "They will have simply put a paver over it. That could be our way in."

"The sewer system?" I asked.

Sir London frowned. "The old sewer system wasn't used for ages. Maybe there's a secret room down there. I don't know, but that's the only hope we have left. Let's go for it!"

"How?"

"First we have to find the tile that's covering up the entrance to the old sewer system. Then we'll pry it off and jump in."

"But which paver is the right one?" murmured Marvin, looking around helplessly.

 Which of the pavers was the entrance to the sewer system under? You can be off by one paver and your answer will still count as correct.

(Difficulty "Ultimate" - do consider checking the hints section in the back of the book.)

MARKET PLACE NEWS

THE MARKET PLACE IN THE 18th CENTURY

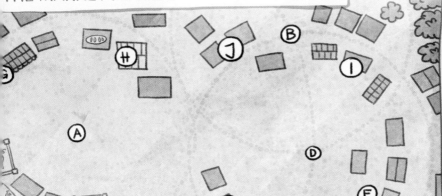

A) Main City Well (preserved)

B) Time Pillar (renovated)

C) Entrance to Old Sewers (sealed with new tiling)

D) Market Fire Hydrant (dismounted)

E) Fishery

F) Meats

G) Vegetables

H) Bakery

I) Wine and Spirits

J) Craftsmanship

K) Animal Livestock

Originally, the market place floor tiling showed three smaller circles of equal radius as well as one larger circle. The radius of the larger circle equals the distance between the well and the time pillar.

NEW TILING FLOORPLAN

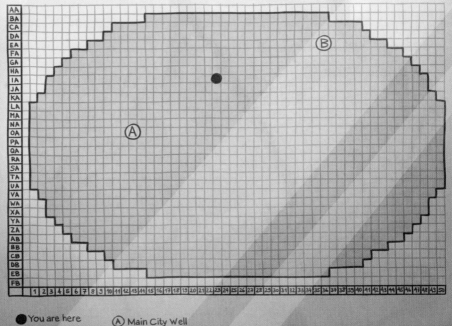

● You are here

A) Main City Well
B) Time Pillar

The market place tiling was completely renewed. You are currently standing on tile IA23.

CHAPTER 23

In Disguise

WE STARED AT TILE BB34 at our feet. It was our best bet, given we could not be entirely sure. "And now?" Marvin asked.

Lilli stepped over to Marvin's side and laid her arm around his shoulder. "If I had some chalk we could play hopscotch."

"Funny," said Marvin, shaking her arm off.

"Okay kids. We need to get in there, and to do that we've got to get rid of the paver," began Sir London.

At that moment, the bells of the church clock rang.

"Boy is that loud," said Marvin. "No-one could sleep through that."

Just as Sir London was about to go on, the clock struck a second time. Sir London furrowed his brow and looked up at the church tower. "It's one thirty. It rings once for every quarter hour. Next it will ring three times."

"One thirty," murmured Lilli, sounding worried. "Hopefully our parents don't notice we're gone."

"They don't know you're here?" Sir London sputtered in surprise.

"Of course not!" and "What did you think?" were our replies.

He stared at us as if we were a few sandwiches short of a picnic. "Then we'll have to stop right now. We'll take a taxi. Where do you live?" Sir London asked.

Lilli wasn't having any of that. "Nobody's stopping anything. We're doing this for my grandpa, don't forget. If we don't find the treasure, he's getting kicked out of his house tomorrow." Lilli's determined tone seemed to take Sir London by surprise.

"But, but, don't you realize..." Sir London stammered in a quiet, squeaky voice as if he wasn't sure whether he should say it, "even if we find the treasure...how are you planning on turning it into money so quickly? The find has to be registered...rights have to be filed...the city might claim possession...then there's museums, scientists..."

Lilli looked at him in disbelief. He stared back at her with big pitiful eyes. An awkward silence prevailed for a few seconds.

"Oh, what the heck," he suddenly yelled, full of determination. "Where there's a will, there's a way!" Sir London waved his hand over Lilli's head as if to shoo away all her worries. "Sorrow be gone. We've got a treasure to find!"

"Oh yeah!" cried Marvin, clapping his hands and bobbing up and down.

"We've got three problems to solve," Sir London went on. "First, anyone can see us here, so we have to become invisible somehow. Second, we need something we can use to smash the paver and third... third we have to find a way to break that stone without waking up the whole neighborhood."

"Break the paving stone without being seen or heard," I summarized our task.

"Is that all?" said Lilli bitingly.

We looked around in silence. Shrugging, Marvin suggested, "Let's take the little construction tent from over there and set it up here. Then no-one can actually see us. There's a pickaxe too. We'll smash the paver with that. We'll only strike when the church bells are ringing, then no-one will hear."

We stared at Marvin, speechless. "What?" he asked, shrugging again.

"Okay, that's what we'll do," decided Lilli and trotted off towards the construction tent. Minutes later we had everything set up, ready to go. Sir London stood with the pickaxe over his shoulder and Lilli peeked out of the construction tent to check the time on the church clock.

"Timmi, give me your binoculars," she whispered. I fished them out of my backpack and gave them to her. "There's someone sitting over there on the park bench. Under the street lamp."

"In the middle of the night?"

"Looks like he's asleep, but..." Lilli adjusted the binoculars. "He may be dressed like a homeless person, but I get the feeling it's just an act. At least I'm sure the clothing is only a disguise. He's definitely not as poor as he's making out."

Why did Lilli think it was a disguise?

CHAPTER 24

The Key

THE FAKE BEGGAR WAS missing a glove on his left hand, which Lilli spotted lying in the rather posh car parked right behind him. Also inside the car lay a bag featuring the same logo as the cup our disguised pursuer was holding.

"And isn't that the car that was outside the hotel before?" I asked.

"Could be," said Sir London.

"Definitely," Marvin said. His eyes grew wide. "We're being tailed!"

"The church bells, the church bells! Smash it!" cried Lilli.

The first blow of the pickaxe already shattered the paver. The bells rang twice more, enabling Sir London to strike two more times. After that, there were only little pieces left, which we quickly cleared away while Sir London held his lower back, groaning.

Lilli watched the windows of the houses surrounding the market place. "No-one woke up. Even the man on the park bench is still pretending he's asleep."

"Look at that," I called out in a low voice. Beneath the chunks of paving stone, a bronze manhole cover with an unusual engraving on it appeared. "Lotterlulu's symbol. It's here!" Sir London said, pointing at a star with a half-moon standing out in the middle of all sorts of other symbols. We all stuck our heads together to look at it.

"Another hot lead," I said.

A short time later we had managed to get the heavy cover off, revealing a pitch black hole. A strange, musty smell hit our nostrils. "Looks like a bottomless pit," said Marvin.

Lilli wrinkled her nose. Sir London, Marvin and I all had flashlights with us this time. But the dim light they produced seemed to be mercilessly consumed by the thick blackness of the hole. We couldn't make out the bottom, only the free-standing ladder which led down into the depths of the cavity. I lay on my belly facing the hole and clung to the edge with my left hand. In my right I held the flashlight.

Slowly, I stretched my right arm further and further into the darkness, in the hopes that the light might find the ground. When I couldn't reach my arm out any further, I thought I could see something at the end of the beam of light. "Hold on to me," I told Marvin and felt him grab my belt from behind. Lilli sat on my legs.

"Careful," warned Sir London, as I slowly lowered my upper half into the black hole. The moldy smell and cool air enveloped me. There was something there. Right at the bottom. It must have been a good eight yards deep. But what was it? It was bumpy. It towered up out of the darkness towards me. What was this thing? I wriggled a bit further down into the hole. Then I saw it. It was looking right at me.

"Pull me up, pull me up!" I screamed. I couldn't get out of there fast enough. I reached up for the edge of the hole with my right hand too, dropping my flashlight, and I saw it momentarily light up the creature staring at me. Seconds later I was freed from the darkness and sat on the ground, breathless, a safe distance away from the hole.

"There's something there. There's something in there!" I stammered. Marvin leaned over the hole and stared down, a curious look on his face. "Marvin, get back," I shouted.

He looked over at me and rolled his eyes. "It's just a statue."

"What?"

"A statue that's looking upwards. Your flashlight is on the ground and it's lighting it up."

I crawled hesitantly over to the hole. Marvin was right.

When, a little while later, we had all climbed down the ladder, our flashlights lit up a room with three passages leading off it. The walls were earthy and the ground was covered with old wooden planks. You felt like you were in a mine, not in a sewer system. There was no stinky stream. But there were all kinds of strange statues and murals.

"Look at all these sculptures," Lilli whispered.

Sir London lit up the statues. "Lilli, get your grandfather's key. I have a feeling it will come into play now. Let us examine these statues. Maybe we can find a secret keyhole."

"I think I see something," said Lilli.

From the front, the key looked like a cross. Can you find a keyhole it would fit?

CHAPTER 25

The Secret Passage

CAREFULLY LILLI INSERTED GRANDPA'S key into the statue's eye and turned it. We noticed a quick, audible click. We whirled around in fright and shone our flashlights into the darkness.

"It came from the wall over there," said Marvin. At first we couldn't see anything. It took a few minutes to find the secret door which had opened only a crack.

"Beautifully fitted, you can hardly see it at all." Sir London ran his fingers along the breach in admiration.

"The treasure, the treasure!" Marvin cheered and the beam of his flashlight darted here and there over the floor.

For a short moment, I forgot the oppressive darkness of the ancient passageways around us and only had an incredible feeling of anticipation. I would have bet the others felt the same.

Sir London crammed his fingers into the crack and started pulling the door open. It was hard work. I jumped in to help him and pulled with all my might. Slowly but surely the almost three-hundred-year-old passage opened up.

❖ ❖ ❖

Marvin shone his light in. "There's a corridor." That was a bit of an exaggeration. The corridor was barely more than a narrow crevice. Its walls were exposed earth and in many spots roots jutted out from them. The crevice was just wide enough that you could squeeze along it sideways.

"Oh no," I said.

"Doesn't look good," Marvin agreed quietly.

Lilli shone her flashlight in his face. "Can you even fit?"

Marvin shone his light back. "Do you even dare?"

Sir London eyed the narrow passage. "I'll go first. You stay close behind me. Understand?"

We nodded. Sir London squeezed into the opening, followed by Marvin, then Lilli, then me.

The crevice was tight. Really tight. Earth tumbled down onto us, getting into every imaginable part of our clothing. Roots grazed over our faces. From somewhere in the darkness above, water kept dripping on us. If there had been spiders, my worst

nightmare would have been complete. We pushed and shoved onwards, yard by yard, minute by minute. The secret entrance soon
disappeared from view.

The air grew stuffier and stuffier. I took a puff from my inhaler. Onwards. For some reason I had a bad feeling. These walls
were suffocating me. I stopped a moment, closed my eyes and
tried to calm down. My breathing was shaky. Lilli and the others
kept looking forwards and didn't notice I had stopped. I'd catch
up with them in a minute. Once I'd had just a little bit longer to
calm down.

❖ ❖ ❖

Something moved. I opened my eyes and stared into the darkness. To my left I heard Lilli and the others, working their way

forwards, far away from me. How long had I been standing here? It must have been a few minutes. There it was again. That sound. It came from my right. Something was moving to my right, moving towards us. Towards me. A scratching and scraping. Something else was squeezing through the crevice.

I had to get to the others. I pushed on like crazy, further and further. It was working. I was making good progress. I could already see Lilli again by the beam of my flashlight. They had stopped. I was almost there.

Lilli turned to me. "Timmi, what is it? Are you okay?"

"I don't know. I think there's something behind me." Then I saw why they had stopped. Sir London stood before an ornately decorated door and examined it in fascination.

There were nine panels on the door, each with a different symbol. Some were normal letters, others came from other languages and still others were universal symbols from maths and physics. Above them stood a riddle:

What is found once in a pirate's ship,

Thrice in the Star Runner

And not a single time in the whole King's fleet?

"Shush, be quiet," I said and stood motionless. There it was. Suddenly we all heard the scratching and scraping coming from the darkness behind us. And we all panicked.

"Quick, get us in there," Marvin yelled at Sir London.

"Get that door open," cried Lilli.

When Sir London pushed on one of the panels, he suddenly screamed, but his scream disappeared just as quickly as it had begun. Beneath his feet, a trap door had opened and he had fallen right into pitch black nothingness.

We shone our flashlights into the hole. It didn't go straight down, it was more like kind of a slide. From somewhere below us we heard a groan. "Sir London!" I called out.

"I'm fine," came a voice from the darkness of the hole. "The door must be opened by pushing the correct panel." The next thing we knew, the trap door slammed shut again.

"Oh no, which one is it?" stammered Marvin.

"Let's hurry," Lilli added, as the scraping from the passage behind us got louder and louder.

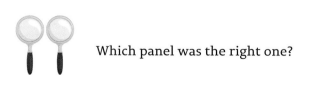 Which panel was the right one?

The Trail of the Guardian

IN SPITE OF ALL the panic, somehow I managed to concentrate. The voices around me became faint. *What kind of riddle is this, Lotterlulu?* I thought. What could possibly be found exactly three times in the Star Runner but not once on some ships of an old king? What are you trying to tell me? There must be some trick to it. And then, suddenly, I saw it. It was the letter "r".

The words *Star Runner* contained the letter three times whereas the words *King's Fleet* did not.

I instantly reached over and pressed the symbol on the door. We heard a click. Lilli and Marvin held their breath and stared at the door. As I pushed on it, it opened up slowly. We quickly slipped through, into the next room, and swung the door shut. In contrast to the narrow pathway which lay behind us, an almost endless dark expanse now stretched out before our eyes. The ground, the walls and the almost twelve foot high ceiling were made from thick, dark planks of wood.

"What is this place?" whispered Lilli.

Marvin shone his flashlight into the darkness. "Looks like a never-ending room."

I kneeled down and ran my hands over the floor. The wood seemed to be ancient. A little damp maybe. The air smelled of it. I shone my flashlight back at the door. The wall it was in disappeared into darkness both on the left and the right.

"Let's walk along the wall," I suggested. "It must lead somewhere."

Marvin nodded. "At least that way we won't get lost."

"Okay, let's go!" said Lilli.

We jogged alongside the wall, following the beams of our flashlights. At any moment I expected us to come upon a fork in the road or something like that, but the wall just went on and on.

"Unbelievable," cried Lilli, out of breath. Only after about another minute did we make out something in the darkness.

"A corner!" said Marvin. "The wall turns left."

"Then let's follow it. We keep going," Lilli decided and we turned left.

"Good grief, it's huge," groaned Marvin.

"Stop," said Lilli and we stood stock still. "Do you hear that?"

Somewhere from the depths of the room we could hear noises. "It's coming from the door," I whispered.

"Flashlights off!" ordered Lilli and we did as instructed. Now it was pitch black all around us. For a short while all we could hear was our own breathing. Then came a click and a creak. The door was being opened. "Whatever was following us is here in the room with us now," whispered Lilli.

"There, look!" Marvin said quietly, although still unable to hide his excitement. "Over there." The beam of a flashlight moved, a little spot dancing through the dark room, far away from us.

"Where's he going?" asked Lilli.

"Not along the wall, anyway," I replied. "Looks more like he's going towards the middle of the room."

"But not towards us, right?" whispered Marvin.

It was hard to tell. But from one moment to the next, the dancing spot of light disappeared.

"Where has he gone?" asked Lilli. "Did he switch off his flashlight?"

"I don't think so," I said. "Maybe there's something else over there, a room or something. And he went in."

"Then he must know his way around."

"Of course," I said. "It must be one of the Guardians from the Dark Power." We strained our ears, but no more sounds came from the darkness.

"If we want to find the treasure, we have to go to the same place as the Guardian was rushing off to in such a hurry." My idea was greeted with silence. I gathered up my courage, switched my flashlight on again and said, "Let's go. This way." We darted towards the middle of the room, treading gently to avoid our footsteps being heard. Soon all we could see by the light of our flashlights was the floor and the ceiling. No walls, no matter which direction we shone them.

"Hopefully he's not standing around here somewhere with his flashlight switched off, lying in wait as we walk straight towards him," Lilli whispered.

"No way," I said. But the thought of it did freak me out a bit.

❖ ❖ ❖

After a few more steps we came upon another wall. This one wasn't straight though, it was curved. We followed it to the left and finally found what we were looking for. Before us stood many statues resembling the ones we had seen before and there were three archways in the wall.

"Each one leads to a different path," I said. This must be where our pursuer's light had disappeared.

"Look at these spider webs," said Marvin, clearly excited.

"Do you know what I think?" asked Lilli.

"Yeah, that those spiders must be giant!" exclaimed Marvin.

Lilli shone her flashlight in Marvin's face, giving him a look that told him not to get on her nerves.

"No? Then you're wondering what they eat?"

"No."

"I am. Then you're wondering where they're hiding?"

"No."

"Guess they hide and wait in the shadows."

"Okay Marvin, probably," said Lilli, shining the flashlight back towards the archways. "But do you blockheads know what I was thinking about our three pathways here?"

"That two of them lead to death!" proclaimed Marvin.

Lilli shone the light back into Marvin's face, who smiled at her, bobbing up and down gently. "Actually, something along those lines, yes," said Lilli.

Marvin stopped bobbing and his eyes widened.

"And we've got no idea which is the right one," I said.

"This is going to be fun," whispered Lilli.

"You know what is fun? Spiders. Spiders are fun," said Marvin. "You know what's not fun? You. You're no fun. No fun whatsoever."

Which archway had the guardian passed through?

CHAPTER 27

The Perfect Hiding Place

WE'D CHOSEN THE ARCHWAY where the spider webs had been broken by the Guardian. Our flashlights bounced off the moist walls of the passage and a thick mist floated around us up to hip height. Lilli darted ahead; I bringing up the rear.

"This is creepy," whispered Marvin.

"It's just mist," I said, trying to sound calm.

"I can't see my feet and the floor's really sticky," said Marvin.

"No it's not. Stop whining," said Lilli.

"But it is, I can feel it too. It's getting muddier with every step," I said, coming to a halt. "It feels as if…" I couldn't immediately pinpoint the sensation. Then it struck me and I yelled, "I'm sinking! Pull me out!"

Lilli and Marvin grasped my left arm as I felt the surface under my feet giving way faster and faster. They pulled with all their might and when my right foot came free, I tumbled and fell to the floor next to them. Here the ground was earthy but solid. Or was it? It seemed to be getting moister and squishier by the second.

"I think the ground's dissolving," I cried, jumping to my feet. "We must have triggered a trap. Run!"

Screaming and yelling, we took off like lightning, rushing along the passageway, leaving a trail of stirred-up mist behind us.

After about a minute a dead end put a stop to our mad dash.

"Oh no, did we miss a turn?" asked Lilli.

"No, I'm sure we didn't," I said, gasping for air.

"We can't go back," said Marvin, stomping his feet on the ground. "I think it's getting sticky already."

"This can't be the end. The Guardian took that passage," I said.

Suddenly there was a loud clatter. Marvin must have stomped on something and had already dived down into the mist, looking for it.

"Oh boy," said Marvin, fully engulfed by the thick foggy layer. "I found gold coins!" He jumped up as if he'd been sitting on a spring, waving a little, blue sack filled with coins in his hands. Although I felt excited, I was afraid we didn't have time to celebrate and immediately ducked down into the mist, leaving Marvin somewhat perplexed. There had to be more. A way out. Then I saw what had caused the clatter. A metallic plate lay toppled over next to another plate holding an old book. A little higher on a small stone pedestal was a third plate. It was empty but featured an inscription. "Know Your Goal" I read aloud. "There's a riddle here." The others came over and crouched next to me.

"We have to put the gold or the book on the pedestal," I said.

"Of course," said Marvin. "Our goal is treasure. So it's the gold."

I had a feeling that wasn't going to be the answer. "What if it's not gold that's the big prize here? Lotterlulu had plenty of that. It's just not special enough."

Lilli nodded slowly. "Yeah, you could be right."

I shone my flashlight on the inscribed plate. "What now?"

"Well, the book then," said Lilli, grabbed it and placed it on the plate without hesitation. Almost simultaneously, we heard a quiet click followed by a harsh crack.

"There!" cried Lilli. The outline of a trap door appeared in the floor and light poured from it into our dark surroundings.

"Why is there light coming out of it?" whispered Marvin.

"I guess that means we won't be alone down there," I answered.

We lay flat on our stomachs and lifted the hatch up just enough to peek beneath it. I'll never forget what we saw. We were in the ceiling of a two-story room whose side walls were made up of bookcases overflowing with old books. A large chandelier with artificial candles hung halfway up, emitting a cozy light. Right beneath our hatch, an ornate, metal spiral staircase swept down to the ground. There was no sign of our pursuer.

We climbed down in silence and when we found ourselves at the bottom, we stared around the room in astonishment. "There must be hundreds of thousands of books in here," whispered Marvin as he looked up and turned slowly in a circle.

"The perfect hiding place," I murmured.

"What do you mean?" asked Lilli.

"All this only makes sense if it was a book Lotterlulu was trying to protect. A special book. What better hiding place than this?"

Marvin sighed. "Who'd read all this?"

Lilli stared at the countless spines in desperation. "How are we supposed to find the book if we don't know anything about it?"

"We know one thing," I said. "It's valuable. So they'd probably go check on it often. I think I have a rough idea where it might be. At least which bookcase it's on and how high up."

"Me too and from up here I can see one book with dust missing on the bookshelf in front of it. Someone has taken the book off the shelf frequently," said Lilli.

Which book was it? (Difficulty "Ultimate" - do consider checking the hints section in the back.)

The Last Warning

APPARENTLY THEY HADN'T CHANGED the position of the book in all these years. You could tell from the scratches on the wooden floor which spot the ladder had been in most often. The steps on the ladder were also more worn up to a certain point. That gave us the approximate location of the book, and there was only one there that had been taken out often, which we could tell from the missing dust on the bookshelf. It was located in the compartment B7.

Lilli only touched the book through a cloth, wrapping it up and bringing it carefully over. Lying on the table like that, it looked harmless, yet we were entranced.

It was small, even smaller than a standard paperback. The sturdy binding was decorated with a blood red border which enclosed a bare, light brown center. Although it seemed to be well preserved, every fiber of the book exuded the spirit of times long past. It was definitely old, very old, from even earlier than Lotterlulu's time. Lilli reached for a wooden ruler, which she carefully slipped inside the book. Inch by inch she lifted the cover.

The edges of the first page looked almost dark brown, while the middle of the pages shone in the original, light color of the parchment. Two words adorned it in an elaborate script. We couldn't tell what language it was, but I'll never forget those words: El

Iksir. Although we didn't know the meaning, we were awestruck at the mere sight of the letters. After all, we knew it must be about a secret that had been closely guarded for centuries.

Lilli was just about to start turning the pages when the chandelier above us suddenly went out and we found ourselves enveloped in pitch darkness again. "Oh no," said Marvin.

"Flashlights, come on, turn your flashlights on!" I cried out, urgently rummaging around in my backpack. A loud crack made me stop and flinch. No-one moved a muscle. Only our breathing, heavy with fear, broke the renewed silence.

Then we suddenly heard another noise. Right up close to us. As if a door was creaking open. We all edged back a few steps, away from the sound. Then silence again. Footsteps! Clearly audible footsteps. The wooden floor creaked. Lilli gave a little cry. Marvin whispered in a trembling voice, "The Guardian. No eyes. No mouth."

The footsteps stopped. But then a deep, unwavering man's voice spoke out so loudly that my legs gave way beneath me and I sank into a crouch. "Never! Never again will you come searching for this book. Never. This is my warning to you. My first, final and only warning." I felt Lilli's hand on my shoulder.

More footsteps. The door creaked again. Silence once more. "Hello?" squeaked Marvin after a few seconds. "Are you still there?"

"I think he's gone," whispered Lilli, who clung on tightly to my arm.

There was an audible click and then the lights on the chandelier flared up again. Soon afterwards it was shining as brightly as before, lighting up the room with its warm glow. We were alone.

"The book," Lilli said. "It's gone!"

"As long as the man is too," stammered Marvin.

My hands were trembling. I sat down for a moment and took another puff of my inhaler to be on the safe side. Lilli and Marvin both looked pale and sickly, as I probably did too. Disappointment was written all over Lilli's face, whereas Marvin's showed relief. When the two of them saw me sitting, they sunk to the floor too. "What now?" asked Marvin. "How do we get out of here?"

"There must be an exit. Maybe there's a hidden switch or lever somewhere here for a secret door," said Lilli, and I nodded in agreement. "Do you see anything that's been moved? Is anything different from before?"

 Where was the secret switch? By the way, it was neither a book nor the globe.

CHAPTER 29

New Hope

WE TURNED THE LAMP downwards and then back to its original position. With a loud click, a piece of the bookcase sprang open a crack. The secret door gave way with a creak, revealing a small room which was almost completely filled up by an infinitely high spiral staircase. Our way out. Accompanied by the beams of our flashlights, we raced up the steps. All we wanted was to get out of here, into fresh air. Out of the danger zone.

Arriving at the top we found ourselves faced once more with a door. We opened it quietly and peered out into a corridor. We seemed to be standing inside some kind of cupboard, which served as a disguise for the secret entrance to the book's hiding place. Careful not to make any noise, we climbed out of the closet. At the end of the hallway the front door awaited us, and we quickly tiptoed towards it.

The door opened easily and we shot outside, not without shutting it gently behind us. We found ourselves right in front of the marketplace, which was bathed in the first light of dawn. We ran across the square, screaming with relief. Now it didn't matter if anyone heard us. Now we were out. Away from danger. Finally free, free, free. We rollicked about until we ran out of energy.

Completely breathless, I fell to the ground and looked up at the sky. It was going to be a beautiful summer's day, you could tell already, even if the sky was quite dark and you could still see stars. What Lilli's grandpa had told us about the treasure came to mind once more: *The treasure is high above, under a tent of stars, on the other side of a moon.*

I turned my gaze towards the others. Lilli and Marvin suddenly looked as if they'd turned to stone; both were staring in the same direction. Then Lilli suddenly ran off.

I followed her with my eyes and saw someone lying on the sidewalk not far from the building we'd just come out of, holding his head. It was Sir London. We all ran over to him and he slowly clambered up. He insisted he was fine and didn't need to see a doctor. Then he told us what had happened.

Apparently he had found a way out and waited for us here. He paced back and forth anxiously for quite a while, and was just about to call the police. Then, just before we all rushed out the front door onto the market place, he suddenly saw a man leave that same building. He was wrapped in a long, black coat and seemed to be in a big hurry. Sir London asked him whether he had a phone he could use to make a quick call to the police, and the man promptly hit him over the head with his cane.

"All I got was this." Sir London held up a piece of black coat material. We all sat on the sidewalk leaning against the apartment building and looking out over the marketplace.

"Then at least we're not going home empty handed," grumbled Lilli sarcastically. And even though it wasn't really funny, we all couldn't help but laugh. We were relieved and happy to have gotten through this adventure in one piece.

It got light quickly; the day was breaking. "But it's such a shame we didn't find anything that could help," Lilli said, sad about the way our adventure had ended. "Grandpa will be out of a home soon." No-one said anything. Lilli broke the silence. "We should go to him. We should be with him when it happens."

All at once, an excited clapping interrupted our sorrow. We looked over at Marvin in surprise. Eyes wide, face beaming with delight, he kept on clapping his hands excitedly. "I've got it! I've got it! We're not going home empty handed! And I am not talking about those old books down in that cellar!"

 Marvin remembered something that had happened rather incidentally a few chapters earlier. What was it?

CHAPTER 30

Lotterlulu's Treasure

MARVIN REACHED INTO HIS left pants pocket and pulled the little bag of gold coins out.

"You stole them?" asked Lilli in surprise.

"No, I just forgot to put them back after you guys were so keen to put the book on the plate."

"Great job!" I cheered and jumped up. "Off to Grandpa's house!" I reached out a hand for Lilli, which she accepted, and I pulled her to her feet.

"You all go on without me," groaned Sir London. "I'll get myself a taxi and follow after you." As soon as he'd said that, we were off.

❖ ❖ ❖

It was still early in the morning when we arrived at Lilli's grandpa's place. Our parents would think we were asleep and hopefully wouldn't miss us. Strangely, the front door was open and we walked in.

"Grandpa?" called Lilli. There was a strange smell in the house. Not like cigarettes, but similar. A strong, bitter tobacco smell. Someone else was here.

"For a non-smoker, your grandpa sure is tolerant," I said.

"He's a gentleman," Lilli told me. "Old school or whatever." She looked up the steps. "Grandpa?" It took a few seconds, then we heard a "Lilli?" It came from upstairs.

We raced up the steps and found Lilli's grandpa in the attic once more. As we had guessed, he wasn't alone. Grandpa sat on a chest and before him stood a stocky man with a moustache and metal-rimmed glasses. It was the representative of the bank who had brought the bad news yesterday. A cigarillo glowed in his mouth and his faced glowed with rage. "Great, now this," he grouched at us.

Lilli threw herself into her grandpa's arms. "What are you doing up here?"

"I was getting out the ownership papers for the nice man. They prove the house has been in our family ever since it was built."

"That's all fine and good," said the man, "but the fact is, you owe our bank a lot of money. So now the house, and the land it is on, by rights become our property. And either you leave voluntarily, right now, or I call the police."

"Not so fast," I yelled triumphantly. "We've got your money!" Marvin threw the little sack of gold coins over to Lilli.

She passed it on to her grandpa. "Here. This is for you. It's from Lotterlulu."

Grandpa's eyes grew wide. "You found the treasure?"

"Not exactly. But at least we found some of it."

The man with the moustache didn't hesitate long, snatching the little sack. "This is unbelievable," he said and glared at us angrily. "Such audacity. Unbelievable."

Marvin and I looked at each other in confusion and shrugged.

"It's not enough," said the cigarillo-smoker abruptly, and cast the little sack back into Grandpa's lap. "At most it's a partial payment. You could get a few days grace maybe, but only if the find really belongs to you. And I doubt it does."

"We found the gold! And an underground den and a library with hundreds of old books that must be worth way more!" protested Lilli.

"Even if that were true, child, things like that all belong to the city. A finder's fee. Maybe you'll get a finder's fee. Just because you find something doesn't mean it belongs to you."

"What's that?" I suddenly burst out. "Has that always been here?"

"What? What do you mean?" Marvin asked the question they were probably all thinking.

I looked at the others, stunned, and stammered, "If I'm not very mistaken, this is where we'll find the real treasure. Lotterlulu's treasure."

Lilli stared at me in disbelief. "What? Here?"

 What made me think we were about to find the treasure?

CHAPTER 31

All or Nothing

"THE TREASURE IS HIGH above, under a tent of stars, on the other side of a moon," recited Grandpa and as soon as we ripped away the first plank of wood with the moon engraving, gold pieces trickled out of the cavity hidden behind it and landed on the floor of the attic. Marvin clapped his hands and hopped up and down, while we all took turns hugging each other. We couldn't believe our luck. The treasure had been hidden before our very eyes the whole time!

The man with the cigarillo stood silently off to the side and twiddled with his moustache as he watched the scene playing out before him. In the end he simply tossed the half smoked cigarillo on the ground and stomped it out. "I don't want to be a wet blanket, but I have to inform you that you'll only get a finder's fee for this treasure too."

"What?" cried Lilli, outraged.

"As of today, the house and the land it is on belong to the bank. Consequently, the treasure does too."

"Wait," said Lilli's grandpa. "The house might belong to you, but not the belongings I have inside it. The armor over there doesn't belong to you either!"

"Correct." The man with the moustache grinned cunningly. "But unlike the armor, the treasure doesn't belong to you, it belongs to Lotterlulu. You only found it. And on our property no less."

We were all speechless. But the representative of the bank was right. It wasn't our gold. Not even the house we'd found it in belonged to Lilli's grandpa anymore. "Maybe there will be a finder's fee," murmured the man as he lit up another cigarillo. "But for now I must ask you to leave. Perhaps I should call the police after all, with so much gold, you never know…"

Out of the blue we heard a familiar voice say, "You couldn't be more wrong."

We looked around in surprise and saw Sir London climbing through the hatch into the attic. "Sir London!" the three of us cried out as one.

"I think I need to explain something here," Sir London groaned. The night had clearly worn him out.

He turned to Lilli's grandpa. "Did you never wonder why the portrait of Lotterlulu has always hung in this house? And where your family got the key you gave the kids yesterday?" asked Sir London. "Even this house has always been in your family. Doesn't it all seem like a pretty big coincidence?"

No-one answered and Sir London cut to the chase. "Well, it's because Lotterlulu settled here in this very building. He put down roots and started a family." He went silent and stared at our questioning faces. "He started YOUR family. You're a descendant from him. Lilli, didn't you ever notice how much you resemble the portrait? The nose? The ears?"

"I'm a descendant of the infamous pirate Lotterlulu?" stammered Lilli.

"You're a pirate princess!" cried Sir London. "Oh, and before I forget – that clearly means that as Lotterlulu's descendants, the treasure belongs to Lilli's grandpa and his family."

Sir London cast the cigarillo-smoker a triumphant look, who growled back, "Yeah, if you can prove it."

"I'm sure we can, but I don't think that will be necessary," Sir London said, making a point to sound calm and casual.

The man bit his cigarillo and hissed through his teeth, "Oh, I think it will be."

"Really?" growled Sir London. "Do you want the whole world to know about El Iksir? And do you want to be charged with assault and attempted murder?"

We stared at Sir London, speechless, and he gave us a sly smile. "I see several clues indicating that this man is our pursuer, the one who struck me down before."

 Can you find one of the clues Sir London was talking about?

A Summer's Day

"THE CAR OUTSIDE THE Hotel Savoy. A whole mountain of half-smoked cigarillos had collected under its open window. Few people smoke cigarillos, and even fewer only smoke them halfway. I bet it will turn out they were your cigarillos."

"Even if they were, that proves nothing!"

"I am not done yet. This morning I was attacked by someone in a black cloak. It was you."

"I sure can empathize with whoever attacked you."

"Maybe you didn't notice, but I tore off a piece of your coat. This scrap here fits perfectly into the hole on your shoulder." The accused was visibly surprised as he peered at the tear in his coat. "Furthermore, the imprint on the bump on my head is an exact match for the pattern on the knob of your cane." Now the man pressed his lips together and stared at Sir London's forehead. "And finally, I bet that package under your arm contains a book. The El Iksir. Since the book is so important to you, I imagine you won't be letting it out of your sight any time soon. Not now that it has been taken from its supposedly safe hiding place."

The representative of the bank was silent. All color drained from his face. He clung on tight to the package. "The book...you're not getting it," he stammered and eyed Sir London.

"I'll make you a deal," said Sir London. "You acknowledge in your records that you received the full amount owing to your bank today from Lilli's grandpa. I won't lay charges and we'll all forget about the book."

For a few seconds, which seemed like an eternity, the man considered Sir London with a nervous look. He seemed to be weighing up his options. His features grew more and more tense, and his pale skin turned increasingly red. The cigarillo crumbled under the grinding of his teeth. Suddenly he pulled a document from his coat pocket, slammed it down onto a wooden case and began to fill it in quickly. After he signed it, he handed the fountain pen to Lilli's grandpa.

None of us dared move let alone speak, as if we might blow it all if we did. We looked on, silent and motionless, as Lilli's grandpa took the pen in his trembling hand, examined the document and finally signed it. As he handed the pen back, he glanced over at Lilli with a relaxed smile and tears in his eyes. She put her hands to her face and looked at him half questioningly, half bewildered.

Lilli's grandpa nodded and whispered faintly, "The debts are gone."

Lilli screamed and fell into his arms. Marvin jumped after her and threw himself into the embrace too. The three of them almost toppled over. I smiled at Sir London and nodded gratefully, to which he replied with a quick, sly wink. Group hugs aren't really my thing, but when Lilli looked over at me, tears in her eyes and a demanding expression on her face, I joined in for a bit.

The creaking beams of the attic floor made us look up. It was the footsteps of the stocky man, who was retreating in silence.

"Didn't you forget something?" I called after him and gestured to his cigarillo which still lay on the floor. The fiery look he gave me showed he was livid. I tried to hold his gaze. I was probably imagining things, or maybe it was the shadows in the twilight of the attic playing tricks on me, but for a second I could have sworn his eyes and mouth turned pitch black. Just as the legend had described the Guardians of the Dark Power. Suddenly I felt funny. My knees shook.

When he finally did turn and quickly went down the stairs, without having picked up his cigarillo, I knew exactly what he'd wanted to say to me with his look. *This isn't over*, he'd told me, and *Look out, we will meet again.* I watched him go, deeply intimidated. Only then did I hear the laughter around me and feel Lilli's hand patting me on the back. And the fear gave way to relief.

Up until moments before, I'd still thought all was lost, but now I found myself overjoyed and surrounded by friends. It was still early in the morning, but you could already tell it was going to be a hot day. Swimming weather. The smell of freshly mown lawns would hang in the air. Somewhere music would be playing. And somewhere, a new adventure would begin.

THE END

HINTS

The chapter hints are listed in reverse order, to avoid spoilers when you read them using a small mirror.

Chapter 31

How did Sir London describe the incident a few chapters earlier? What could be use to identify the attackers?

Chapter 30

Lotterjulju had described where the treasure was hidden in a little riddle. Do you remember it?

Chapter 29

Marvin said he didn't mean the old books we just left behind. He meant something unmistakably valuable like jewelry, gold, diamonds or something similar. But what?

Chapter 28

Compare this picture with the one from the previous chapter. The change is clear. If you're not sure, then you've probably got it wrong.

Chapter 27

The more often you use something, the sooner it will shows traces of use. Let's take three steps to solve the puzzle. First, can you find a clue that might give away which section of the bookshelves labeled A to F had been visited the most? Second, can you find markers that indicate which of the shelves numbered 1 to 17 had been visited the most? Don't forget to take into account how tall an average person is. Then look for a book with dust missing on the bookshelf in front of it.

Use a mirror to read!

Chapter 26

The neighbour couldn't walk between the statues without leaving a trace.

Chapter 25

The riddle was really quite sneaky. It was more about the words than their meanings.

Chapter 24

Sir London was right when he guessed the statues would be a part of the solution. Look carefully at their eyes.

Chapter 23

Lilli wasn't just looking at the homeless man at that stage, she was looking at the surroundings too.

Chapter 22

Have a look at the three small circles and the big circle, all of which are marked with dotted lines in the picture showing the old marker place. Try to redraw them on the picture of the new paving plan by using a compass. How can you find the radius of the big circles? What do you know about the radius of the small circles?

Chapter 21

The text of the riddle linked two words in each sentence, as if there were a connection or a link between them.

Chapter 20

Marvin had discovered a pile of clues that normally takes more than a few minutes to accumulate.

Chapter 12

There were lots of symbols on the map. Did one of them have something to do with Lotterlulu?

Chapter 13

I noticed something was missing in some places. It couldn't have been a coincidence.

Chapter 14

The heavy chandelier was tied to the ceiling with a tightly stretched rope. A second rope wound loosely around the first. It didn't seem to be used at all.

Chapter 15

To this day, many booby traps are triggered by the victim unwittingly touching or cutting hidden cords.

Chapter 16

The modern day object that gave it away is known almost the world over.

Chapter 17

What kind of black powder was that by the oil lamp and where did the trail lead?

Chapter 18

To be able to tie the knot, we didn't necessarily need a light that lasted long.

Chapter 19

Of course, from time to time pirates liked to raid other ships. To do that, they approached the ship in question on the high seas and then had to somehow manage to pull that ship close enough to their own to be able to board it by storm. They used the object I was looking for to do this.

Chapter 11

Maybe the portrait was rolled up.

Chapter 10

I guessed he had stolen the portrait of Lotterlulu. I came to that conclusion by comparing photos that were taken on two different days. I noticed two differences in the pictures.

Chapter 9

The receptionist didn't want to tell Lilli the room number, but she gave her another crucial piece of information. And Lilli secretly suspected that its London would drip the winner of the private reading himself.

Chapter 8

You might find the answer more easily with a pen.

Chapter 7

Did you know that, with a little bit of practice, people can use typewriters without looking, even blindfolded? But most of all, the cane behind the man looked unusual.

Chapter 6

What time was it at that stage? What was going to hap-pen in the next ten minutes? Does anything suggest that the woman would soon leave her desk?

Chapter 5

Maybe Lilli's grandpa had done something else with the glass. Maybe that's why we couldn't spot it right away.

Chapter 4

We want to know who visited Grandpa one day earlier. First, of course, we need to know what date and day of the week the previous day was. You will hint a bit in the story. Can you see anything on the table that gives a clue to the date?

Chapter 3

According to the riddle, the object (or part of it) must be able to move, and it must have something to do with war and peace.

Chapter 2

Lilli must have noticed something that would change within a short period of time. Something temporary. Like a cup of hot cocoa that goes cold quickly.

Chapter 1

Marvin didn't say whether the way in was a door, a chimney, an open window or a mouse hole. He also didn't say he had already found it. Maybe he only noticed something that suggested there was another way in. But what?

I wish you lots of fun reading this book :)

ACKNOWLEDGEMENTS

First and foremost, I would like to thank my wife Anja for supporting me in following my passion and picking me up when times get tough. Love and kisses.

❖ ❖ ❖

I would also like to thank my whole family who have read this book throughout its various development stages and supported it in numerous ways.

❖ ❖ ❖

Special thanks go to Markus Bruckner for being so enthusiastic about this story, to Nicolas David for his belief in my ability to deliver quality content and to Martina Denzer for two motivating Timmi Tobbson cups.

❖ ❖ ❖

Thank you to Cindy and Tracy for putting up with a long and unconventional production process and for delivering such high quality work. You guys are the best.

❖ ❖ ❖

Special thanks go to mum for being the best mum in the world and to dad for telling me to do what I like best.

FUN FACTS

This book contains a puzzle which is unrelated to the story and involves all thirty-one main illustrations. A hint can be found on the cover. Go to www.timmitobbson.com if you think you have the solution.

❖ ❖ ❖

Some of the main illustrations contain references to friends and family of the author.

❖ ❖ ❖

The Academic Archives email address will actually answer if you send in a job application.

❖ ❖ ❖

Thankyou to Hans Jürgen Press, whose adventure *The Black Hand Gang* was among my favorite things to read as a kid and inspired me to create Timmi Tobbson just as much as the countless classic adventure games I enjoyed on my Amiga and PC machines.

❖ ❖ ❖

At one point in this story an artefact is mentioned by name. If you search for this name online, you may get a better understanding of why it might be considered very valuable.

ABOUT THE AUTHOR

Jens I. Wagner lives with his beloved wife, who is expecting their first child Emmelie Amilia at the time of writing, and two big orange cats right at the edge of a forest near Frankfurt, Germany.

He earned a master's degree at Oxford University where he loved being part of the Christ Church College community.

Jens is a fan of all kinds of fiction ranging from *Sherlock Holmes* to *Star Wars*.

Do you like this book and want to help spread the word?

At the time of writing, we have no big publishing house to support us and it is you, and only you, who can make all the difference. Here is how you can help:

1. You can go to timmitobbson.com and register as a fan. This way I can keep in touch with you, share exciting news, ask for your opinion and give you a glimpse behind the scenes.

2. Leave a review on the internet platform of your choice. Every review helps us to gain visibility, increasing the chances of a sequel title. Reviews are super important.

3. Tell your friends, teachers, bookstore, library, book club, etc. about Timmi Tobbson. Every bookstore and library should know about and stock this book.

Should your school, book club or any other group order ten or more copies, go ahead and tell me (write to timmi@timmitobbson.com). Let me know how many copies were ordered and I will send you just as many book plates (stickers that go inside the book) with my real (not printed) signature on them! Attention: The availability of book plates is limited. Please go to www.TimmiTobbson.com to see if we still have enough left.

Whichever way you choose to help: Thank you so much!

All the best, J. I. Wagner